William Isaacs Loomis

The Anti-Newtonian. Incidents and Facts in My Life

William Isaacs Loomis

The Anti-Newtonian. Incidents and Facts in My Life

ISBN/EAN: 9783337056117

Printed in Europe, USA, Canada, Australia, Japan

Cover: Foto ©Raphael Reischuk / pixelio.de

More available books at **www.hansebooks.com**

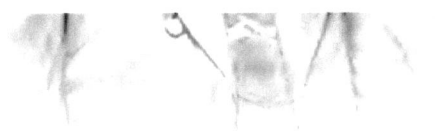

Wm Isaacs Loomis.

THE ANTI-NEWTONIAN.

INCIDENTS AND FACTS

IN

MY LIFE.

BY

WILLIAM ISAACS LOOMIS,

Pastor of the Antioch Baptist Church, 264 Bleecker Street, New York.

New York:

THOMAS HOLMAN, PRINTER, CORNER OF CENTRE AND WHITE STREETS.

1869

GOD THE SAVIOR IS MY GLORY.

In the *Life of Flavius Josephus*, written by himself, he boasts of somewhat better blood in his veins than that of ordinary mortals, resting his claim on a lineage of illustrious relatives, and a motherhood in a line of priests and kings.

Being an ordinary mortal in the commonwealth of men, I rejoice in that the one blood of mankind flows through my veins. The beaming smile of my mother, which shone on my infant face, was a reflection of the smile of the Queen Mother of Eden, and in it could be read my pedigree—an offspring of God. Such a descent of birth and blood, made not less sacred on account of ignorance and sin, is glory; and animated by it, my brothers and peers of the race, in the use of their godlike powers, may rise to a distinction which their Creator will delight to honor.

After so long time from the creation of man, and while the philosophers are so abundantly satisfied with Newton's demonstrations of his *System of the World*, I announce to my countrymen and the world discoveries of facts of nature in the celestial science of astronomy which are anti-Newtonian. An appeal from Newton's *Principia* to the facts of nature constitutes the foundation of my arguments; and assuming that some may ask: Who is he? I have concluded to say a few words in reference to myself, course of life, and the way in which I was led to the conclusion that it was my duty to oppose the philosophy of Sir Isaac Newton, and give to mankind the natural law of the motions of the heavenly bodies.

Births.

1. On a Christmas Day, 25th of December, old style, 1642, a child was born, an Englishman, at Woolsthorpe, in the parish of Colsterworth, in Lincolnshire, and named Isaac Newton. He became the father of a new philosophy. At his kingly nod erring astronomical savans of the past were unthroned, retired, and laid away in silence, to gather dust on their lips in a long repose. Under his all-grasping scrutiny, Nature appeared to be no longer willing to withhold the long-sought-for and knowledge-coveted cause of the motions of the heavenly bodies, but delivered it to the man she most signally delighted to honor.

2. On a Christmas Day, 25th of December, new style, 1810, a child was born, an American, in the city of New York, in Orchard Street, and named William Isaacs Loomis. This child of God and of nature was moved to investigate the works of his heavenly Father, and being, as he believes, divinely led in a new and true way, discovered the origin of gravitation, and the way in which the God of nature generated the motions of the celestial bodies.

Early Recollections.

The gloom of experienced wretched poverty hangs over the early days of my remembered being, and the pleasures of infanthood made

charming by the ordinary comforts of life I never
knew.

Once I nearly perished by fire. Then a watery
grave yawned in vain to swallow me up. Afterward the dangers of a rocky precipice entangled
my feet, and gave momentary threatening of dash-
ing out my life. The hazards of the way culminated in the premature discharge of a musket, the
deafening report of which assured me that there
was less than one step between me and death.
Thus I was made acquainted with the alternations
of safety and danger, with the experience of being
scantily and plentifully fed, that all these changes
might be sanctified in the adorning of a blessed
life. In the epoch of Immanuel's advent and
humiliation, his divine sufferings and agonies gave
a repletion of interest to the glory of his triumph ;
and, in the annals of eternity, what has been or can
be so redounding to the praise of the Godhead as
the life of the Lamb of God from Bethlehem to
Calvary? What if Death did wed Christ on the
cross, and Death and the Prince of Life became
one? What if, by the unthrobbing heart of Jesus,
hope lay weeping in dismay? The resurrection!
Yes, the resurrection of our Redeemer assures us
that all was not lost. Have ye not heard of that
terrible moan of triumph when Death, in darkness,
put his crown on the dead Christ, and the lips
which had given life to the dead were closed in
silence? All this ruin but preluded a reign of life
eternal for the suffering children of earth, and to
it the ragged and hungry, the sinful and suffering,
may look through Christ for a release from every
sorrow.

Education.

My first teacher was an elderly matron, whose wrinkled face wore an air of sad sobriety, unenlivened by a smile; but she was full of teacherly goodness, and wolfish words, the twin brothers of profanity, never defiled her lips or heated her blood. Under her instructions the class of which I was a member advanced to a first reading lesson, which was the first chapter in the New Testament. The Hebrew names of the memorable worthies occurring in this first reading lesson were to us insuperable obstacles, which compelled every one of the class to change his base every minute during the lesson. My second teacher was a bear-man, whose hugs and slaps gave him a life-long place in the memories of those who were put under his care, and suffered the astonishment and surprise incidental to his unexpected thumps and punches. At this time our school books were a Spelling Book, a Bible, used as a reading book, and an Arithmetic. My first writing lessons were with a stick in sand. Atlas and Geography were to us unknown books. By a happy incident I got hold of a Grammar, opened to the verb "To love," and committed to memory the persons of the verb in the indicative mood. Not understanding what the persons of the verb, nor indicative mood, nor what love did or could have to do with Grammar, I cast the book aside as wholly useless, and that was my first and only lesson in grammar till I was over twenty-one years of age. Attached to our school was a gymnasium, under the personal and sole direction of our teacher, to the benefits of which the whole school was eligible, without a

money charge. The agility of the pupils was
brought into the most lively being by a fishing-
pole, fifteen feet long, a mahogany ruler, thirty
inches long, and other beautiful appliances, such
as a flat hand, a doubled-up fist, and booted foot,
interchangeably used, never failed to enlarge our
muscles, and give us a keen sense of lively times
and an enlargement of our lungs. But what
appeared to be an initiation into mathematical
skill, though unknown to us at the time, was our
gyrations, our master for the time being in his
own person the centre of attraction. In these ex-
ercises the master would take us by the hair of the
head, or by both ears, or by our coat collars, and
then we could describe the trajectory of a comet
in less time than by geometrical construction, and
our whirling descriptions of areas of conic sections
produced the deepest conviction of the accuracy of
our demonstrations in the mind of our teacher;
and when we encountered the centrifugal force of
our master's boot, from the tip of it we flew off on
a tangent, and the period of my first eight years
was marked on the records of time.

The Second Eight Years.

About the beginning of this period I was employed by a very respectable hotel keeper, at
whose bar liquor sold for six cents per glass, the
measure of which was half a gill and no more,
and his charge for board was four dollars per
week in advance. These then first-class prices
raised this hotel to great respectability, and secur-
ed for it a superior company of customers. In
this hotel I experienced my first promotion in the

activities of public life, and was elevated to the
dignity of scullion in the kitchen and sub-bar-
tender.   In this two-fold office the world opened
before me for the first time with plenty to eat, and
plentifully varied drinks.   My dream of life was
enlivened by the music of gobbling turkeys and
cackling hens, while the sweet incense of hot rolls
and smoking cups of coffee regaled my sense of
smell.   Now, indeed, had come to me a jubilee of
uproarious joy, a millennium of good things without a night, for we were accustomed not to go to
bed till morning, and my translation from penury
and want to a bountiful larder and bar and money
drawer of my new home was all I could desire,
and more than my young visions of plenty had
ever dreamed of.   I now mingled with a class of
men whose examples were in keeping with that
terrible proverb : "Eat and drink to-day, for to-
morrow we die ;" men whose darkened minds pre-
vented their knowing and doing aught but evil,
and among them I learned the following poetry :

> "Friend of my soul, this goblet sip,
>   'Twill chase that pensive tear ;
> 'Tis not so sweet as woman's lip,
>   But, oh ! 'tis more sincere.
> Like her delusive beam,
>   'Twill steal away the mind ;
> But, truer than love's dream,
>   It leaves no sting behind."

As if it were not enough to rob woman of her
sincerity, and crown her mistress of delusion, the
men of our house took pains to teach me that
womanly virtue was only a beautiful name, mar-
ketable at a given price, and sometimes as cheap
and cheaper than a glass of brandy.   This wild
assault on the charity of heaven in the gift of

womanly virtue was but the outspoken effect of how deeply depraved were the men of such sentiments, and, if warrantable, lead me to inquire what kind of creatures had they in their chosen wives and mothers !

A Redeeming Feature.

One time, and only once, a minor came to our bar and called for strong drink. At this time the master of the house and his lackey were behind the bar, and one of the most beautifully formed of young men, with rosy cheeks, entered the barroom. He was, as near as I could judge, about eighteen years of age, richly attired in broad-cloth, a diamond breast-pin glowing on his bosom, in his hand a gold-headed cane, and, standing before the bar in the stateliness of royalty, he called for a glass of brandy! "Boys can not drink brandy at this bar; you may have a glass of beer," was the reply of my master. The young man looked on us for one moment, his face covered with a tinge of red anger, then in silent contempt he turned from us and went his way, to be seen no more at that bar. But what would have been the measurement of his astonishment had he known that behind that bar stood a boy who, when the grass was growing on his master's grave nearly half a century afterward, would bring that beautiful youth into notice, and rehearse : "Boys can not drink brandy at this bar; you may have a glass of beer."

A Change.

From the enjoyed scenes of a joyful life with men whose great aim was to drive all kinds of

care away, I was taken and put in the employ of a
New York broker. The respectability of his family,
the lady-like deportment of his daughters, the quaint
nature of their mother, and the stern mandates of
their father, opened to my view new scenes and
contemplations. This part of my life, so unlike
anything in my former experience, made me un-
easy with its cold sobriety, and hate its moral
bearing. Without one drop of anything to cheer
me as I had been cheered with life among the
jolly drinkers, living less bountiful and varied than
when in my hotel home, tended to make a moral
life a burden to be avoided, and the hope of being
myself again as I had been was not to be indulged.
When among the sons of Bacchus I ranked in
dignity with them ; and now to be compelled to
acknowledge myself inferior to those I served, and
wear the yoke of their restraints, was too much for
my endurance. Invoking the third change in my
life it came, and I was advanced to the office of
sub-clerk in a grocery store on Long Island, where
the best of liquors sold for three cents per glass
with a cigar thrown in, and the cigars when re-
tailed sold three for one cent.

The Young Lover.

The most remarkable event of this period of my
life (about my twelfth year) was my falling in
love with a rich young lady whose years were
about a third more than mine. What made me
love her so I do not know ; but this I know, I loved
her. Now that first grammar lesson, of which I
have informed you, stood before me in the verb "To
love ;" in a captivating force that bowed me abso-

lutely to the service of a new-born passion, and
now understanding the verb and also what love
had to do with grammar, I wished to conjugate it
until unwearied death would tear asunder the conjugal bond. I had seen many a rose-bud of lovely
beauty like her blooming as the flowers of Paradise along the pathway of life, and because they
bore the divine image they were more exalted in
the scale of being than the angel Gabriel. He in
his princedom is nothing but a servant; but they
were queens of heaven, born to be the daughters
of Immanuel, to inherit eternity, and sing the
anthem of his holiness in heaven. All these left
me as unimpassioned as the rose of summer jeweled
with a dew-drop of the morning, its leaves gather-
ing strength and beauty as it drinks the rays of the
rising sun. Then, for the first time in my life, I
experienced a passion of loving-kindness, pure as
the sacrificial flames of holy priests at God's altars,
and sinless and unselfish as a mother's love. Had
I been a Peri, I then felt prepared to repass the
beautiful gates of Eden, and Cherubim with flam-
ing sword, instead of smiting a sinner, would pre-
pare the way to welcome a lover; but, alas, the
earth earthy clogged my way, and not knowing
what else to do, I never told her of my adoration
of the beautiful, but embalmed her in the young
lover's dream.

In this grocery my knowledge increased, and it
was not long before I was able to take four drams
a day without a scruple. Here I became a companion of men who claimed to be the truly Scrip-
ture temperance men, who never scrupled to take
a dram, and always for their stomach's sake.
What to the uninitiated might appear droll, this

society of men would commend the sanctity of
their lives to the diligent observance of church
members, men who claimed to be pure-minded and
religious. Of this company who frequented our
store, some of them had graduated from State
prisons, and others were from the respectable to
the lowest walks of life ; but the use of the three
cent rum sling slung all distinction to the four
winds, blending us in. the closest brotherly union.
When the most perfect of our customers were congregated in the store by night, as they often met,
under the operation of the spirits they became sur-
prisingly learned and eloquent, and in these times
the law and religious commentaries of lawyers and
divines were transcended in legal lore and sacred
criticism, and were consigned to an age of darkness.   This company of immortals praised their
principles of unwavering virtue and priceless honor,
from which they could not be persuaded to part,
except the telling of a lie would do more good
than the truth. Such a sacrifice might be endured,
if it did not degenerate into a habit.   These patrons
of the rare graces also concluded that it was wrong
to take strong drink only when you wanted it.
Never to fight and quarrel, only in manly self-
defense ; never to curse and swear, only when it
became necessary to exhibit a proper resentment
in righteous indignation.

One more plunge in the ways of evil and change
of employment, and the scene opens in a gambling-
house, in which I was installed game-keeper and
general runner. Occasionally it came to my mind :
There is something better to be enjoyed than I am
in quest of. But what could I do or know in my
surroundings? No men of God were to be found in

the paths I pursued, and darkness, deep and awful, buried me in its gloom. Paganism had its false gods and altars of devotion, and times for worship, but among the class I had moved in for years not even the name of a false deity was known, but to be profanely used in cursing, and the cultivation of godless sensibility absolved from all future dread of woe. In my new vocation I at first experienced delight in new scenes, surrounded by well-dressed men. Often seeing splendid jewelry and the possessors of large sums of money, I hoped for bright days to dawn in showers of gold, and the reveling joys of a gambler's life ; was growing to be a lover of pleasure and hater of God; but despite the abscence from the good, the resulting destiny of a life wasted in sin would haunt me like a ghost of evil. At one time I was as godless in my thoughts as though atheism had succeeded in obliterating from the facts of nature the evidence of the existence of the Creator, and then would rush in upon my soul so deep a sense of guilt, that the miseries of the lost seemed to be my impending lot. I had known of the dying unpardoned gambler in the grasp of the *mania a potu*, suffering in his delirium the anticipated horrors of damnation, and trembling with the thought that my chosen path led to that same result, and fearing lest I at last should find a place and burial in that hell that my companions had so often thundered in my hearing, I forsook the gamekeeper's life, and determined to be something. I knew not what, or when, or how.

Improvement.

In the seventeenth year of my life I was indentured to Mr. Michael V. Cregier, of the city of

New York, to learn the art and mystery of piano-forte making. Under his care and instructions the barbarian boy was inducted in ways of morality, and advanced in well-being and mechanical skill. My will being in almost complete submission to my master and his wife, I tendered to them the most perfect obedience, and the yoke of their restraints I suffered with patience and to much profit in after-life. Not one of my former employers but had suffered some through my pilfering, though not enough to balance my claim on them for unrequited labor; but during my apprenticeship I did not steal to the value of a cent. So determined was I to lead a different life, and so complete my conquest over some of my former sins, that honesty and obedience became pleasant and desirable duties, which I rendered to every one entitled to my service.

Marriage.

On the fourth of July, 1776, our republican fathers, of blessed memory, called the world to a new cause of joy, by their declaration of freedom, and then began a nation, whose course was destined to gather under its shield a greater number of happy families than had ever before found pleasant homes in freedom's bower. On the anniversary of that great day, July 4, 1828, feeling a desire for the enlargement of my freedom, and the joy in hope of making one of the happy families of the land, I asked an orphan girl of the name of Hannah Marshall to take a walk with me and enjoy the pleasures of the day. During that walk our hearts became so entangled as never to be separated, and, on the 23d of February, 1829, Mr. and Mrs. Wm.

Isaacs Loomis began to be among the actualities of married life. I had heard of the charms of solitude, and a sigh for a lodge in some vast wilderness; but the solitude of being alone, with your sweetheart with you, and the lodge in the wilderness of conjugal felicity, was more than poetry to me, and nearer paradise than ever before. The fruit of this marriage had been coveted by kings, who had counted children a more glorious portion than crowns and dominions, whose hopes, however royal, were vain; but our lot was to see eight kindlings of God's immortality clothed in the vestments of our flesh, reclining on their mother's bosom for the nourishment of life. Six of our children were brought up at our table, surrounded with the enjoyments of a pleasant home, and were trained to read the Bible in course as a part of our daily family devotion. Our first child (deceased) and fifth child (deceased) and eighth child were daughters. Gather the rose-buds of infant beauty, and transplant the gems of immortality to the Savior's crown, was the decree of the Almighty, and our first and fifth child fell from their mother's bosom into the Redeemer's arms. Our fourth child, when he had attained the years of a man, had his hopes in this temporal life destroyed by the angel of death. But there is a record called the Lamb's Book of Life, in which, if a name be written, it is the name of an heir of the blessings of eternity, whose well-being is identical with the well-being of the Savior. This son having asked for and by faith obtained a name and place in that Book, by confessing Christ before men, and having been baptized into his name, what can await him but "Come, ye blessed of my Father," when Jesus

shall come the second time without sin unto salvation?

Conversion.

My wife was naturally opposed to frivolousness;
and belief in the good truth of God, as set forth in
the divine Scriptures, was all-commanding, and she
earnestly desired to be made a follower of the
Lamb; but I was indifferent to that holy estate,
while I did not care for Jesus, led me recklessly in
the way that leads at last to the lament of the loss
of heaven. At her request I was induced to attend
a meeting. In giving my consent, I thought only
of the novelty of the occasion, and went solely for
the fun of seeing the antics of the simpletons, and
to laugh at their foolishness. Esteeming the ideas
of sport and frolic supreme, there was not a place
on the earth, not excepting God's sanctuaries, too
sacred for its enjoyment, and in this way possessed
I found myself surrounded with the solemnity of a
company of men and women, whose blood-bought
souls worshiped God with power. When the final
amen of that meeting, its services, and God's work
in it, had passed into history, my Creator heard me
confessing my sins, and saw me feeling the need of
Jesus. A change for good and God-ward had come,
the light appeared, and henceforth the bond-slave
of sin resolved to battle for life, liberty, and eternal
happiness. Nearly four months afterward, a morning bright, resplendent with the heavenly light of
the Sun of righteousness, broke in upon the darkness of my mind. My soul, receiving the spirit of
a freeman in Christ, was quickened into spiritual
joy, and from that hour to this Jesus Christ has
been the repository of my heart and hopes.

Call to the Ministry.

Not long after the beginning of my acquaintance with Jesus Christ, and companionship with the Lord's people, I was moved by the Holy Spirit, who had brooded over me and made me a child of heaven, to preach the gospel. The idea of God calling such a poor unlearned creature as I was appeared as practicable as his calling the born dumb to sing his praises, both of which are within the possibilities of divine power; but that he could use me in the illustrious work of winning souls by preaching was with me a great question. I had read and learned so little of anything that was good and true, had been so lately brought into the light and knowledge of salvation, that if I preach the gospel with the Holy Spirit sent down from heaven God must create a new way in this desert of my mind, and lead me in a wilderness in which I had no capacity to walk. While I was deliberating in wonder, the passage, "All things are possible to him that believeth," inspired me with strength and hope. I soon began to experience that a heart given to the dear Savior, warmed by his love, and moved by it with love for sinners, was one of the means to build up the glory of Christ among men, that the excellency of the power should be by the Spirit of God, and not in the excellency of words which man's wisdom teaches. Being anxiously desirous to set forth the glad and heaven-ennobling tidings of salvation in the most tender and effectual manner, I resolved to educate myself to a degree that might glorify my Creator, and cause some of my race to hear the word of God in its munificent gifts of promise to the sinful on their believing. Auxiliary

2

to this great aim of my life, I purchased a Bible,
Buck's *Theological Dictionary*, and Dr. A. Clark's
Commentary on the New Testament. The no-book
course of so much of my former life had induced
in me a perfect dislike of books, and the incident
weariness of study was slavery indeed. My capacity for compositions was limited in my new field
of thought to but few words, then followed a hard,
tedious time of thinking with the gain of a few
words more. Encompassed with these difficulties,
I laboriously pursued my way to the prize before
me, over a more than corduroy road of ups and
downs, rising at four in the morning to study the
word of God by lamplight. To enlarge my means
of giving to the heirs of glory gems of thought that
would tend to make them wish they were shouting
with the harpists of heaven, I acquired some knowledge of the English, Hebrew, Greek, Latin, French,
German, and Spanish languages ; and each one of
said languages has contributed to increase the
powers of my mind and the emotions of my soul.

Torturing Trial and Triumph.

In deference to human authority, which is supported by the best of reasons, I applied for license
to preach ; and my first rebut was : "What a fool
you are ! Your forehead is so low that thoughts
have no room to jump up and down in your brains."
I was, however, admitted to the dangers of trial
sermons, and the next stinger was : "William, there
is no use of your trying to acquire the art of
preaching, your articulation is so bad, you chew
your words to such a degree that it is difficult to
understand you." One more lunge, right through

my heart, and the agony was over. My friend and companion, an old and holy man, whose gentleness of manners made him appear lovely, had recommended me for license to preach, and on our way home from one of the appointments of my course, opened his mouth and said: "William, I am sorry that I have had anything to do in commending you for the office of a preacher, you are mentally incompetent to comprehend the truth of the gospel, so as to communicate it to the edification of men; you will be ever learning, and never able to come to the knowledge of the truth." This was to me agony indeed, because in my meditations I had prophetically foreseen success crowning my efforts, and kings and priests of God and the Lamb sitting at my feet in transports of delight, hearing my announcement of the heaven-derived truth as it is in Jesus. Then looking on my congregation, I saw their penitent tears, and heard their cry for pardon, hope, and heaven, and then to be told by the man whom I esteemed to be my best earthly man-friend, "You are mentally incompetent to become a minister," was like a chalice of poisoned hemlock to my hopes. Oh, how it did wring my heart, and ring in my ears, and hung the black pall of desolation on my fondest, holiest aspirations! I had been a vagabond in sin, and had seen men of wickedness make a chowder of virtue and honor, and devour it as if the feast had been one of purity; and those guilty revelers in evil had never questioned my mental ability and eligibility to be one of their chosen number for a life-course of sinful pleasure. I had passed from death unto life, and going up the hill of hope, a voice from the celestial world urged me with, "Go

preach the gospel;" and in the surroundings of
those deeply solemn circumstances, my heart given
up to the work, to be told : " You can never make
a minister of Christ," was sounding the loss of the
crown of my hope.   One more opportunity was
granted me to try my gift, which was to be the
last before my case would be called up by those
who had it in their power to bind on earth what
God had bound in heaven, or, through their ignorance, throw to the winds my application for their
indorsement of the divine decree.

It was in 1832, in the city of New York, the
cholera was raging, and sorrowful sadness in its
carnival of gloom sat throned on every face.   On
our way to the meeting-house, I said to my friend
who accompanied me in my preaching trials : " You
will take the lead in the service, and I will follow you."
He replied : " No ; because you know, William,
that it is uncertain whether you preach five minutes
or twenty.   Therefore you will take the lead, and
if you break down I will come to your support."
We reached the meeting-house, and our eager eyes
were filled with the sight of a crowd.   Many of the
hearers were clad in robes of deep mourning, and
all felt that the wing of the angel of death over-
shadowed us.   I rose to speak to a company of men
and women, whose tearful eyes and grief-stricken
faces seemed to speak to me, and say : Young man,
if you have any words of consolation, say on ; for
God's sake, give us words of comfort.   Eyes of the
creatures made in the divine image never before so
glanced on me.   And by one of those extraordinary
manifestations in which it was shown that the excellency of the power was of God and not of man,
the whole assembly was bathed in tears.   For nearly

two hours, I charmed that congregation in a heavenly place ; then during that service I did hear the
kings and priests of God and the Lamb shouting
hallelujah ; I did see sinners in tears, imploring the
God and Savior of us to have mercy on them, and
give them hope and home in heaven. We were on
our way home once more, and my friend said : " William, I will give up my former opinion of you.
Your words are understood by your hearers, your
brains are big enough ; you do understand the
truth, and can communicate it understandingly, and
all my fondest hopes would be gratified if I could
change prospects with you."

In process of time I was examined by a regu-
larly constituted council of Baptist ministers ; passed
a creditable examination ; was counted worthy to
take rank with the ministers of Jesus, and Rev.
Duncan Dunbar, pastor of the Macdougal Street
Baptist Church, preached the ordination sermon. I
projected a course of studies, embracing that of
medical science, intending, if the opportunity ever
came to hand, to use it in procuring a degree of
M. D. I studied a plurality of authors on anatomy
and physiology ; numerous authors on diseases of the
lungs, stomach, and bowels ; and on some of the diseases which render so many of human kind invalids
through life. I read treatises on their cause and
treatment by Allopaths, Homœopaths, Hydropaths,
and Eclectics, and the knowledge derived was of
the most essential benefit to me.

So far in my ministry, I have whirled through
many changes and been pastor of fifteen churches.
In one revival fifty-eight converts came to Jesus,
and in another fifty-two. In one period of three
years one hundred souls were introduced to the

knowledge of Jesus, and I baptized them; and but
for the opposition of other parties, I have reason to
believe that the above numbers would have been
three times as large. In another revival we lost
more than we gained; that is, because we were the
poorest, least honorable, the greater number of our
converts joined a richer and more popular church,
leaving us to lament the loss of those who, in joining where they did, were lost to all usefulness
among the multitude they joined. In the year
1840 I began a translation of the New Testament
from the original Greek. In the progress of my
work I became understandingly convinced that the
translators of King James's version, which has
come to be the generally accepted English Bible,
had rendered some of the passages of holy writ in
such simplicity, power, and beauty, as to forbid
even the hope of a greater degree of perfection.
Being in communion with the original Scriptures,
it gave to me a power and insight to justify a
comparison with it and certain translations; and
using the attainments, it was made to appear that
some of the passages which had been rendered by
the king's translators were put to shame when
placed in comparison with corresponding passages
in the Rhemish (Roman Catholic) Testament and
Douay Bible. Advancing, I was electrified with
divine delight, in learning new beauties of the inspired Greek, which the king's translators had not
introduced into their version, the knowledge of
which could only tend to make the people of God
love their God and Savior and their Bible more
intelligently. A CORRECT TRANSLATION WOULD
HAVE DISCLOSED THE KNOWLEDGE OF

The Orbit of the Earth.

The translators of the commonly received English Bible, otherwise known as King James's version, finished and gave to their nation their copy of the English Scriptures A. D. 1611. The reader may learn from the chronology and fact, that if the Hebrew writers of the Jewish Scriptures had, by virtue of the divine inspiration by which they were guided, made any allusion to any one of the heavenly bodies moving in or having an orbit, the above translators, if of the school of Ptolemy, their error perverting their understanding, could not understand what was meant, and consequently would render their text accordingly, and the fact of nature, a planetary orbit, would not be brought to light. This, I claim, was the case, and that the prophet Isaiah was the first man to intimate the fact of the ORBIT of the earth. I further aver, that when we shall be favored with a translation that shall as nearly as possible equal the divinely inspired originals, it will be seen that the God of nature, and the God of the Bible, the One I AM, in respect to the truly natural sciences, inspired to a certain degree the prophets and apostles in their allusions to the facts of nature, and that they opened the way to the knowledge of the truth of nature as well as they did to the knowledge of theological truth.

History.

The prophet Isaiah flourished about eight hundred years before Christ. He taught in Hebrew a fact of nature, and brought to the knowledge of his countrymen the orbit of the earth. Pythago-

ras flourished about six hundred years before
Christ. He taught his countrymen and others
that the earth has an orbit; but the teaching was
denounced as false, and its discloser was counted by
his countrymen a fool or madman. After this, for
about twenty centuries, the dogma of a fixed earth
generally prevailed, and the most intelligent of
men gave the untruth of astronomy as hearty a
welcome as ever has been accorded to the Copernican-Newtonian Astronomy. About the year of
our Lord 1500, Copernicus, an ecclesiastic of the
Roman Catholic Church, and also a mathematician,
announced his discovery of the orbital motions of
the planets, and in 1543 he informed Pope Paulus
III. that he had kept his book, which contained an
exposition of planetary motions, by him for four
times the nine years recommended by Horace.

In 1666 the discovery of universal gravitation
was made by Isaac Newton. For the want of this
or some other force it was not possible to give a
geometrical demonstration of the motion of the
earth in an orbital path, nor the law of its motion.
Seventeen years after this, or in 1683, Newton
sent to the Royal Society, in London, his laws on
the orbital motions of the primary planets. In
1684 Newton assured Halley that the orbital motions of the primary planets were demonstrated
most perfectly. Never before, in the history of the
world, had such a result been reached, and never
before had men's eyes been opened to see so nearly
the truth. From the forementioned dates it follows, that, while the translators of our common
English Bible had opportunities to know of the
Roman Catholic Copernicus' announcement that
the earth moved in an orbit round the sun, they

were too early, by more than seventy-three years,
to avail themselves of any of Newton's revelations
of science to help them in understanding those
parts of the inspired word of God which refer to
the celestial science of astronomy. Hence, when
the translators came to the Hebrew text, Isaiah xl.,
23, which was destined to give to mankind the in-
timation of the existence of the orbit of the earth,
they were at a loss what to do. None of them are
known to have been believers in the Copernican
theory; they were, if anything in this science, followers of the Ptolemaic system, and it is incontro-
vertibly certain that they had never heard of nor
seen a geometrical demonstration of the earth
moving in an orbit; they were all in their graves
before Newton gave it to the world.

ISAIAH xl., VERSE 23.

"It is he that sitteth upon the circle of the
earth."

The above passage is emphatically astronomical,
and should have been rendered, "It is he that sitteth upon the orbit of the earth;" and thus justly
rendered leads to the result that Isaiah was a
prophet of God, and grand primate of nature, in
teaching the fact of the existence of the orbit of
the earth. Now, suppose the translators of King
James's version had, unwittingly or otherwise, instead of giving the text as they have, rendered it:
"It is he that sitteth upon the ORBIT of the earth;"
what an eye-opener it would have been to the
learned of that day; and what a help for Newton
to have referred to the translation and to this Hebrew text of Isaiah to confirm his demonstration,
that the earth, according to God's inspired book,

moves in an orbit. However obscure such a rendering might have been to the men of 1611, the men under Newton in 1684, the true men and the good men would have seen it shining in a glorious array of brightness, and, clasping the Bible afresh to their hearts, would have thanked God that its light disclosed a fact of nature two thousand four hundred and eighty-four years before Newton demonstrated it to the satisfaction of men. It is admitted that the translation as contended for would have been very mysterious to the men of 1611, and also unintelligible to the world of English readers; but what of that, could it have been more so than was the saying of Job, that "God suspends the earth in the open space?"

The Marvelous.

The God of the Bible is the author of the creation, and hence because he inspires in religion, leaving us not to the cogitations of our own ignorance, but specially illuminates us to do his will, I incline to the opinion, and think it reasonable, that he may make a philosopher in the same way that he does a Christian, by special illumination, inspiring and revealing to such the knowledge of natural astronomy. The cautious, while assenting to the possibility of such a revelation, would most likely question its existence; but God did make mechanics by special inspiration and revelation, and pollylinguists on the day of Pentecost, and the probability of his making an apostle of nature is within the limits of a just expectation. In the book of Exodus, chap. xxi., you may read that Bezaleel and others, by special inspiration and revelation, were made lapidaries, workers in wood and gold, and all kinds of mechanical craft, in order to be able to construct the tabernacle, ark of the testimony, and mercy-seat ; without doubt, if I give the celestial credentials of my call, I may indulge the hope that there are living men who will be benefited by my revelations of the way of the Lord in nature.

About the time of the autumnal equinox, in the year 1846, being at that time pastor of the South Adams Baptist Church, in the State of Massachusetts, and occupying a dwelling-house, now owned by Hon. Daniel Upton, I sat alone in the dining-room of our dwelling in the midst of the evening, meditating in reference to what next I should undertake to advance me in the ways of truth. My loneliness and the quiet of near nine P. M. in a country place was favorable to my longing to know more. My state of mind was much intensified by there coming upon me an exceeding thirst for another deeper drink of the waters of the true philosophy which so ennobles the human mind, and opens the ways of God to the perception and understanding of his children. Under the excitement of that thirst I mentally inquired : "In what direction shall I go in pursuit of an increase of more knowledge ?" And a voice answered : "Go STUDY ASTRONOMY !" The singularity of this way in calling me to a study so entirely new to me was very exciting ; and being awed into inclination to obey, and the belief that something good would come of it to my race, without conferring with any one, I resolved to follow the path in which I had been so mysteriously called to labor in, and a life-long work had begun. The next day I went into

the village of South Adams, to the cabinet work-
shop of Deacon Elisha Ingraham, and was aided by
him in constructing a model with four arms, each
one of them two feet long, two inches wide, of
board thickness, and at right angles to each other.
Within an inch of the outside ends of these arms I
inserted wires, six inches long, to support balls
which I cut from the posts of an old bedstead ;
mounted them on the wires, to represent in one
view the places of the earth at the beginning of
the four astronomical seasons of the year, and
placed a candle in the centre of the model to represent the sun.   In this manner prepared, I anxiously waited for the shadows of evening and that
great first philosophical night of my existence.   It
came ; and the darkness falling so gently on the
clear atmosphere permitted the stars to shine in
the pomp of their twinkling glory, and, also, in the
centre of my model, in the plane of the centres
of the four balls the centre of the light of a tiny
candle was graduated, so that the flame of the
candle might shine as nearly as possible on a
hemisphere of each one of the balls.   However
insignificant my model to represent the earth and
its motions, and the tiny candle to represent the
sun, by their agency I was about to enter into a
vision of the creation, the amplitude of which is as
immeasurable as the eternity of our heavenly
Father, and its grandeur the imprint of his being
and power.

My First Experiment.

I looked for the north star, which was sufficiently near the north pole of the heavens to answer
the purpose, bent the wires of the model, so that

their upper ends pointed to the star, the wires coinciding with the line of direction, and by this means I was enabled approximately to mount the balls of the model on axes, having inclinations corresponding with the inclination of the axis of the earth, and from the representation I learned how much the axis of the earth is inclined from a perpendicular line, and how the prolongation of the earth's axis, north and south to the stars, constitutes the axis of the heavens, around which the whole starry heavens appear to move in the time of a revolution of the earth on its axis.

Second Experiment.

I began to revolve one of the balls (call it a globe), representing the earth, around the candle representing the sun, being very careful to keep the north pole of the globe pointing to the north star during the entire revolution of 360°, and the knowledge of the parallelism of the earth's axis dawned on my eyes and mind.

Third Experiment.

I then placed the ball, its north pole pointing to the north star, so that a line joining the centres of the flame of the candle and the ball would be perpendicular to the axis of the ball, and now the light of the candle shone on one half of the ball from one to the other of its poles, like the sun shines at the time of the equinoxes on the earth. This opened the way to see the truth of nature, and in imagination I enlarged the candle to a sun, the ball to the earth, and placed myself in the open space, and by the eye of my mind I saw the

sun shining on the day of the autumnal equinox
sidewise on the earth, illuminating one of its
hemispheres from pole to pole, excepting refraction, while the other hemisphere of the earth was
in darkness. This was as clearly demonstrated to
my mind as if I had with my eyes of flesh beheld
it. What moments of impassioned rapture I then
enjoyed! The glory of the facts of nature shone
on my path where all had been dark before.

Fourth Experiment.

I then placed the four balls in position on my
model, their north poles pointing to the north star,
and the distances of the centres of the globes from
each other were 90°. I then took a position facing
the north star, and placed my model before me as
above described, and in one view I saw how the
earth was placed in the beginning of each one of the
seasons of our year. Right before me one of the
balls, with its north pole illuminated, and its south
pole in the dark, showed me how the north
pole of the earth, on the 21st of June, is illuminated, and its south pole in the dark. I then
looked to the next ball on my model, and like as
the candle shone on one of its sides, and both its
north and south poles were illuminated, so in
nature, on the day of the autumnal equinox, in
like manner the sun shines on the side of the earth
from pole to pole. I then looked in the order of
the circle to the third ball, the candle shining on
its south pole, but its north pole was in the dark,
and this showed me how and why the earth, on
the 23d of December, presents its south pole to the
rays of the sun, and its north pole is in the dark.

Fifth Experiment.

I then moved one of the balls on its axis in connection with the orbital motion round the candle, which produced a miniature representation of the grand work of nature ; and as the light of the candle at every instant changed places on the ball at the point or line where light and darkness met, so does the line where sunlight and darkness meet on the earth change every instant. I was, in this experiment, enabled to see why the point of the sun's rising and setting are variable, and what proportions of the earth, and also its parts, are illuminated from day to day throughout the year, and why the light of the sun for one instant twice in the year shines from pole to pole, and how to determine the vernal and autumnal equinoctial points. Continuing my observations, I transferred the motions of the ball of my model or representative earth to the sphere of the stars, and lo, I discovered that the daily accelerations of the stars was not due to the orbital motion of the earth, and that fact of nature led to the result that the sidereal revolutions of the planets, as avowed by Kepler, and demonstrated by Newton, are not to be found among the facts of nature. On that memorable night, as its midnight moment flitted by, I was in possession of the key of nature, which, if properly and understandingly used, would open the temple of God's universe, and disclose to man a better knowledge of its God-built chambers in a new system of the world. I felt as if the phantom of a new order of the starry world was calling me to put on its garments of order, and place it in its beautiful array before the men of my race, assuring me that I had discovered the elixir of intelligence. The way of toil lay open before me, and the success within my reach.

I had resolved, on an early and considerate deliberation, never to write a book. At this period I scorned even the idea of imitating anything that had been done in the way of book-making, and then claiming to be its author. Originality alone made me abandon my anti-book purpose. This originality of conception involved and set forth in my book,—the thought of being the first man of the human race to explain the cause of the celestial motions,—the first gospel minister to say to the Church of the Lord of all worlds: "Behold the order of your God and Savior!"—the first American to say to his countrymen: "Rally round the flag, boys, and march in the van of science, leading the nationalities of the earth, and stand sentry over these discoveries,"—so animated me, that the book was written.

My book is commended to the reader. The great features of it are contrary to the teachings of Sir Isaac Newton; and a comparison of the facts of nature with the doctrines of the *Principia* is the wedding supper of intelligence, to which I particularly invite my countrymen, and then hope to marry them to the facts of nature. The following particulars constitute the value of my book:

1. Discovery of the origin of gravitation.

2. That gravitation is not universal.

3. That the force which moves the planets round the sun is not centripetal force.

4. That the force which carries the heavenly bodies round the sun was originally projectile motive force.

5. The reason why the planets move eastward round the sun is given.

6. The laws of motion, which were employed by Newton, in his resolution of his system of the world, are demonstrated to have been without existence.

7. A new theory of the motions of globes; in which it is proved, from the entire passivity of matter, that the doctrine of the equality of the angle of the incident and reflected motions of globes may or may not be equal, according to the manner of the impress of the force. The revolutionary nature of this part of my book is worthy of the attention of every lover of truth.

8. I have not only shown the cause of the earth's motions, but have brought to light the cause of the rotation of the earth on its axis, which fact has never been accounted for in a reasonable way by the Copernican-Newtonian astronomers; nor is it possible for any astronomer of the present accepted system to do so.

9. I have demonstrated the orbital and axial motion of the earth by an original argument, the most perfect and convincing, independent of all the arguments and demonstrations hitherto relied on.

The Glorious Indeed.

From the time of the introduction of man to the contemplation of the beautiful and majestic in nature, on to the time of three years before the birth of the illustrious Newton, not a transit of Venus had been witnessed by any of the earth-born race of men. What is further remarkable, the tables which mathematically predicted the times of the transits were in error. Astronomers, in their blindness, had forced figures, and forced geometry to testify to their misunderstanding, and all of these were proved to be wrong. About three years before the birth of Newton, an English boy, by the name of Jeremy Horrox, possessed by a deep-seated love of the sublime in knowledge, detected the errors of his astronomical fathers, constructed new tables, from them predicted the time of a transit of Venus, and at the expected moment Horrox sees Venus transiting the sun's disk. I have thought that there have been moments of thrilling interest, when a great event was of sufficient interest to excite heaven and fill its inhabitants with rapture. Was not this one of the events so glorious and worthy as to command the rapture of every servant of the Lord in heaven and on the earth? It was, indeed, a moment of glory as God looked on his child—this infant of a moment observing the first historical transit of Venus. He would not, he could not, and did not, withhold his notice and smile at the instant his godlike child marked the beginning of the epoch of the observed transits of Venus. A comet, at the time nameless, was seen in its wonderful, awe-inspiring, and celestial majesty flying through the expanse, and laying under tribute the admiration and fears of all observers. Of those who observed this comet, the most prominent was an Englishman of the name of Halley, and he predicted the time of its next appearance, which would be, in the course of events, some time after his death. In respect to which he said: "My countrymen, I shall be numbered with the dead when this comet appears again; and when the eyes of the world greet its reappearing, tell them an Englishman predicted its advent!" Fame has its reward, and now that comet bears the name of Halley's Comet, and at least one of the celestial visitants has become, by the discovery of its reappearing, annexed to the mental empire of Great Britain. Call to mind the unwearied Kepler, toiling on during a score of years to reach the goal of his hopes. His anxious cares had culminated in what he believed to be a transcript of nature's wonderful, mysterious facts. He had gained the happy, proud eminence in which nature owned him as her teacher, and henceforth his dictum will be law for all the nations of the earth, and also for all ages. He had examined the archives of nature, deciphered her hieroglyphics, and prepared them to be translated into a hundred tongues, so that all might read and hear of the wonderful works of God. The pen d-r-o-p-s from his fingers. The (his) book is written. He reposes for a moment in the silence of devotional awe; mentally surveys his field of work. On wings of light he flies round the orbits of the planets, beholding their order and their distances and motions, and then gives utterance to: "The book is written! I will give way to my sacred joy. If I find a reader now it is well. If not, if I find a reader one hundred years hence, it will be well. I can afford to wait a hundred years for a reader, since God has waited six thousand years for an observer."

I now appeal to you, men and women of our nation, to reward my claims with your attention. Belonging, as I do, to you by birth; devoted to your holiest and best interests for time and forever, it becomes me to place the new views of nature before you in such a way as to secure your assent by the force of truth. Then you can understandingly admire the way of the Lord in nature, and your convictions of the truth will rest on the firm base of nature's facts.

My Philosophical Argument.

IN observations of the celestial motions I learned, that the centre of the apparent yearly sun could not transit the same star at the beginning and close of the astronomers' sidereal year of the sun, the apparent diurnal revolutions of the stars precluding the possibility of such a result. Hence the times of the sidereal years of the planets as given by Kepler must be false also, for he founded them on the assumption that the stars have neither real nor apparent motions, and the assumption being untrue, Kepler's conclusion is of a like nature.

The laws of motion which the philosophers had adopted as sufficient to account for the motions of globes in any direction being inseparably connected with the Newtonian force of universal gravitation, (which force not existing) I found to be incompetent for the uses of nature, and I supplied the want by my discovery: That a single projectile sidewise impulse impinging on a globe would as surely urge the globe in the direction of a curve line, as would the same force if directed in a line through the centre of the globe urge it in the direction of a right line.

The matter of the Universe was originally passive, being naturally without power to move itself.

This passivity excluded the possibility of there residing originally in matter such a force as Newton's assumed force of universal gravitation.   The force of gravity by which the matter of any revolving sphere tends to its axial centre originated in the rotary motion of the sphere, and hence the force of the gravity of the matter of a heavenly body is equal to its weight ; and the measure of that weight always determined by the rate of the axial rotation of the spheroid.

According to Newton, the mutual attractions of the gravities of a bale of cotton weighing 400 lbs., and the weight of the whole earth, are in proportion to their respective masses.

If this was or is so, a force a little superior to the whole force of the attraction of the whole earth would be required to lift the bale of cotton away from the earth's surface.   This is so contrary to experience and observations of all bodies with which we are acquainted by handling, that we have the right to conclude that the Newtonian theory of mutual attractions of all bodies is without the pale of truth, save when two lovers are mutually attracted to each other, and then it is not in proportion to the respective weights of their bodies, but the intensities of their affection.

It is worthy of notice, that La Place, Newton, and their disciples, say nothing about the gravity of matter arising from its absolute weight before it was started into motion, but speak only of the gravity or relative weight of it while subject to the force of axial rotation.   The density of matter is never altered by motion, but its mass or weight may be.   On this account we shall be able to prove that matter may be divested of its entire weight, and consequently of its entire force of the gravity of its mass.

Let us assume the density and the absolute weight of the matter of the sun and planets to have been equal to each other before they were set in motion, and then learn what the force of gravity is, how originated, and how the weight of matter may undergo changes, its density all the time being without change.

When the matter of the earth began to turn on its axis, it encountered the centrifugal force arising from the axial rotation, which reduced the absolute weight of the matter of the whole earth below the measure of its density. The change which took place consequent upon the resistance of the centrifugal force arising from the axial rotation, determined the present weight of the matter of the earth, and also its gravitating force ; and because of this change, what can be more evident than that the present relative weight and gravity of the whole earth did not originally inhere in its matter, but were caused by the force of rotary motion ? Hence the conclusion is fairly reached, that the present gravitating force of the earth did not exist coeval with the existence of matter, nor before the beginning of the earth's rotary motion.

A decrease of the rotary motion of the earth would tend to increase the gravity of its mass, but an increase of the rotary motion would tend to decrease the amount of its gravity. These variations of axial rotations show how matter may be impressed with any measure of gravity, be passed through every possible change of weight to 0, and the density of the matter all the time remaining intact.

Suppose three globes, D, E, F, of pure silver, of equal diameters, at equal distances from the sun; the axial motion of D twice as much as E, and F half as much as E. The matter of these globes, opposed by their varying centrifugal forces, will vary in the nature of the cases, for the weight and gravity of F will be greatest, E less, and D least, but their densities will be unchanged; and a portion of silver that would weigh exactly 16 ounces on globe E, will weigh more on globe F, and less on globe D.

Let us now advance to learn how the particles of a globe may be without attraction for each other, and the matter of the globe be without weight.

Suppose a globe of gold moving in free space, the velocity of its rotary motion tending to equilibrium. In such a state, the particles of the globe will press neither way among themselves, being nicely balanced by the centrifugal force of the rotary motion, and the whole globe will be without weight, or, which is the same, destitute of gravity.

Newton assumed that all matter is pervaded by a force of gravity which is distinguished from its weight.

If such a force was coeval with the origin of matter, like its density was, what can be plainer than that Newton did not even mention it? In fact, did not discover such a whole force! His discovery was: that of the gravity of matter when opposed by a centrifugal force, (!) which is less than the absolute weight of the matter.

Again: if a force of universal gravitation inheres in matter, how did it come to pass—by what oversight did Newton fall headlong in error, and substitute the gravity of the matter of the earth, which is known to arise as an effect of the earth's rotary motion, for that of universal gravitation? What a substitution! What a mistake!

Once more : if the dogma of the universal gravitation of matter is true, then the matter of the earth must be subject to two forces of gravitation. One arising from the rotary motion of the earth, and exactly equal to its relative weight. The other, the inhering force of gravitation, and exactly equal to the absolute weight of the matter of the earth. But two such forces involve an absurdity; and here, plainly seeing that Newton mistook the former for the latter, we have the means at hand to point out his error.

Mutual Attractions.

MY experiments to test the measure of the force of the attraction of the whole earth on certain bodies on its surface, which explode the Newtonian theory of the mutual attractions of all bodies.

First.—A body of iron, weight one hundred pounds, slipped from the hands of a man and fell to the earth. Now, if the attraction of the mass of the whole earth on the mass of iron is as the attraction of the iron on the earth, the attraction of the earth will exceed that of the iron by as many times as one hundred pounds will divide the number of pounds contained in the earth. Newton affirms this to be so, and were the affirmation true, all the men in the world could not lift the iron from the earth's surface. Let us see. The man stoops down and lifts the iron to the place from which it fell, and this lifting demonstrates that the attraction of the whole earth on the iron is less than the

strength of a man. In this experiment we have
the disproof of the mutual attraction of the bodies,
and the mutual attractions of all bodies are equally
baseless.

Second.—An ounce of iron lay on the earth's surface. Schools, colleges, and universities teach that
the earth attracts the ounce of iron with a force
equal to the weight of the number of ounces contained in the mass of the earth. Wishing to determine the measure of the force of the mass of the
earth on that of the iron, and that of the ounce on
the earth, I procured a horse-shoe magnet, having
an attractive force of one ounce and a grain.
When I so placed the magnet that its force could
act on the ounce of iron, it flew from the surface of
the earth, and, giving in its adhesion to the horse-
shoe magnet, was by this medium lifted away from
the surface of the earth. This is a clear and sen-
sible demonstration that the force of the gravity of
the whole earth on the iron was less than 17
grains.

Third.—If the earth lay on the surface of the sun,
a force a little superior to the weight of the earth
would suffice to lift the earth and remove it into
space, and then at the earth's distance from the
sun, their mutual attractions (if assumed to exist)
must be altogether overcome by the superior force
of the earth's momentum, and hence the perturbations of the heavenly bodies as an effect of universal gravitation is baseless. And because the momentum of the moving bodies of the solar system
is a force vastly greater than the weight of the
bodies, the latter must be subjected to the former,
and therefore not a force competent to control the
motions of the heavenly bodies.

But suppose the utmost tension of a string to represent the gravitating force of a 32-pound shot. Then let each one of the many times the mass of the earth may be divided by 32 pounds be represented by a like string. Then let all these strings be twisted into a cable to represent the assumed gravity of the earth to hold the 32-pound shot to its surface.

Now, if the 32-pound shot is held to the surface of the earth by said cable, do you not perceive that a force more than equal to the whole force of the earth's gravity is required to lift it from the earth's surface? But the force of a boy will suffice; and the reason is this: there is no mutual attractions of bodies in proportion to their respective masses.

In Herschel's *Outlines* (442) he makes the utmost tension of a string equal the gravity of the mass of a body; say a string the tension of which will equal the gravity of a 32-pound shot.

D. Olmsted says: A 32-pound ball moving 6,250 feet in a second of time, has a momentum of 200,000 pounds. Therefore the force of gravity will be overcome by the force of momentum in the proportion of 1 to 6,250.

The Earth's Momentum.

HERSCHEL says the mass of the earth is to the mass of the sun as 1 to 354,936, but the momentum of the earth arising from its mass and velocity is greater than the whole of the assumed gravity of the sun's mass, and hence it is too weak a force to counteract the force of the earth's momentum, and it and the projectile force combined compose a force too great to be balanced by the mere force of the assumed sun's attraction.

The mass of the sun has been assumed to be 500 times greater than the mass of all the other bodies in the solar system, and the astronomers suppose that the sun is dragged about as much by the attractions of the planets and other bodies as it drags them about by its attraction. Suppose 500 men on a rope pulling against one man on the other end of the rope. How absurd to say that the force of the one man sufficed to pull the 500 men one five-hundredth of the way toward him, and just such an absurdity is involved in the Newtonian Law of Universal Gravity and Planetary Perturbations. (See *Principia*, Book III., Proposition XII.)

The absurdity will be not a little amplified by Herschel, who says: An effect of the mutual attractions of the earth and sun is the circulation of the sun around "a point 267 miles from the sun's centre." Now when it turns out that the one force of the weight of the earth will drag the combined force of the weight of the sun (which is 354,936 times greater) around a point 267 miles distant from its centre, then the force of one man will suffice to drag 354,936 equally strong men toward him, and when this of the men and that of the earth and sun shall be esteemed the exact truth with respect to gravity and the strength of the men, then any theory can be welcomed as infallible science.

According to Newton, the tendency of the gravity of the matter of the earth is in lines directed from the surface to the centre of the earth, and not along and across the diameters of the spheroid;

also, that the gravity of the earth's mass is directed
outward toward the sun. But how can the earth
have a whole force of the gravity of its mass directed inward to its centre, and a whole force of
the gravity of its mass directed outward toward the
sun ; involving the idea that the matter of the earth
possesses an amount of gravitation equal to twice
its mass. Unless you accept this as true, you have
no use for Newton's Law of Gravitation ; and if
you still insist on its truth, please tell if it is not
like a wind that has the power to blow on the same
line in exactly opposite directions, in the same and
in every continuous instant. When the planets Earth and Venus were on opposite sides
of the sun, the force of the gravity of the
sun was assumed to be directed against the
earth, and also at the same time the whole
force acted against Venus in an opposite direction,
involving the singular agglomeration of the whole
force of the sun's gravity flowing inward to its centre, and the whole force flowing outward directed
to Earth, and the whole force flowing outward
in an opposite course directed to Venus, making
three forces, or three times as much gravity as
could arise from the sun's mass.

Newton, in his theory of gravitation and parallelogram of forces, to account for the orbital motions
of the celestial spheres, adjusted the centrifugal
force of each one of the heavenly globes to an
equality with the force of the gravity of the sun's
entire mass ; requiring as many distinct centrifugal
or projectile forces as there are bodies in the solar
system. Each one of the forces to equal the whole
attraction of the sun on each body, its density and
the square of the distance always considered. What

a multitude of forces! How can the sun furnish them?

Again : Newton assumed that the expanse on all sides of the sun was filled or pervaded by the force of the sun's gravity to an extent equal to the spherical space occupied by the light of the sun. Let us admit this, and then our conclusion will partake of the nature of an axiom ; for the sphere of the sun's light is to the bulk of the earth, as the sphere of the sun's gravity is to the mass of the earth. Hence the earth can not be acted on by a greater proportion of the gravity of the sun, than the part it holds to the whole extent of the field of the assumed sun's gravity, all other bodies must be subject to the same true reasoning, and therefore because any one of the heavenly bodies bears so small a proportion to the expanse filled with the sun's light, and the mass of any one of the bodies bears a less proportion to the expanse assumed to be filled with the sun's gravity, it is the perfection of human reason to conclude that some other force than that of the sun's gravity originated the orbital motions of the heavenly bodies.

Motions.

I HAVE communicated to a top whirling and forward motions, and saw the top advance orbitally in the curve line of a spiral, and when the top reached the centre of the spiral its orbital advance was arrested, but the whirling of the top on its point or around its axis, being retarded only by the resistance of the air, continued until exhausted by atmospherical resistance. From this we may be able to perceive how like motions were impressed on the sun. (See pages 77 and 78.)

The Sun's Motions.

1. THE motions of the sun having been generated by a sidewise impulse, he moved forward in the
direction of a curve line of a spiral, and orbitally
advanced to the centre of the spiral, at which point
he finished his orbital career.

2. The same force which caused the forward motion, precipitated the matter of the sun around his
axis with a velocity tending to equilibrium, and
there being no interference with the rotary motion,
it is perpetual.

3. The matter of the sun, being in a state of
equilibrium, will press neither way, being nicely
balanced by the centrifugal force arising from the
sun's axial rotation, and such a globe I fully believe
the sun to be, the particles of its matter without
attraction for each other, its mass without weight,
and without any conceivable kind of gravity, and
its centre, the true centre of the world.

These reasonings carry conviction to the intelligent mind ; and the dogma, that the orbital motions
of the planets are due to the mutual gravitations of
the masses of the sun and planets, is seen to be as
chimerical as is any known error of the ancients.
The wise among men will be constrained to seek
some other way not liable to so many destructive
objections. Which way of nature I have discovered, and invite you to enter this glorious path, and
see and learn the long sought for cause of the motions of the heavenly spheres. Farewell, thou Law
of Universal Gravitation. Retire from the unbound-
ed field of space and worlds of light over which
thou hast reigned like a god, lulling to rest the in-

quiry: Why move the heavenly orbs in curve line paths? Thy destiny is finished, and now I pray thee do homage to the truth, and let the disclosed knowledge of a RIGHT LINE IMPULSE to urge a globe in a curve line be thy mandamus to unloose the swaddling bands by which thou hast bound the works of God. Take off thy all-grasping hand of gravitation and let the heavenly spheres assert their liberty to move unaided by thee.

Solar Parallaxes.

NEWCOMB'S SOLAR PARALLAX.

In 1867, Simon Newcomb, Professor of Mathematics, United States Navy, published, "*Investigations of the Distance of the Sun, and of the Elements which depend upon it.* From the observations of Mars, made during the opposition of 1862, and from other sources, forming Appendix II., to the Washington Astronomical Observatory for 1865."

On page 29, Simon Newcomb says: "The mean equatorial horizontal parallax of the sun is $8''.848$ with a probable error of $0''.013$, corresponding to a mean distance of 92,380,000 statute miles. For astronomical purposes, the value of $8.''85$ may be taken as a round number of hundredths having equal weight with the above concluded value."

My Solar Parallax—$8''.8485$.

In my analysis of Newcomb's parallax of the sun, I proved that the angle which the equatorial radius of the earth subtends, seen from the sun's centre, is $8''.8485$, and corresponds to a mean distance of 92,380,416 miles.

In my studies to bring the solution of any equatorial horizontal parallax within the pale of common arithmetic, I obtained the following results :

1. The arc of the equatorial horizontal parallax of the sun, or of any one of the planets, is the arc of a circle, the semi-diameter of which is the mean distance of the sun or planet from the earth's centre.

2. The arc which subtends and is the measure of the parallactic angle of the sun, or that of any one of the planets, in linear measure is the same as the linear measure of the earth's equatorial radius.

3. To prove an equatorial horizontal parallax, compare the linear measure of the arc of the parallactic angle, with the linear measure of the earths' equatorial radius, and if they coincide, the parallax is reliable.

4. The substitution of the linear measure of the earth's equatorial radius, for the linear measure of the arc of the parallactic angle of the sun is justified on the ground that there is no appreciable difference between the sine and tangent of the angle of the solar parallax, and consequently there can be no difference between the arc and tangent ; and the same is true of the parallactic angles of all the planets. But should some pedantic or inexperienced scholar think there is a difference, notwithstanding the smallness of the parallactic angles of the sun and planets, a trial of the case in actual work will convince the most skeptical of the truth of my statement.

Example to find the sun's mean distance by single proportion in common arithmetic :

As the arc or angle of the sun's parallax..........8".8485
Is to the circle in degrees........................360°
So is the base line of the parallax.............3,963 miles
To the linear measure of the circle, 580,442,786.91301
miles÷3.14159=184,760,833 miles in the diameter of the
circle÷2=92,380,416 miles in the radius of the circle, and
this is the term of the sun's mean distance. (See pages 91
and 92.)

This change in the solar parallax involves a change in the real diameter of the sun, and I have the honor of being the discoverer of how to find the term of the sun's real diameter in the fourth term of a single proportion in common arithmetic. (See pages 88 and 89.)

Example to find the real diameter of the sun in the fourth term of a single proportion in common arithmetic. (See the "rule" on page 89.)

As the arc or angle of the sun's parallax..........8".8485
Is to the sun's apparent diameter...................32'.4"
So is the base line of the parallax.............3,963 miles
To the real diameter of the sun.............861,707 miles

N. B.—The term of the sun's apparent diameter I selected from the American Nautical Almanac for 1864.

Also, Newcomb's parallax of the sun changes the value of the sun's mass, taking the mass of the earth as unity to equal 326,800 earths, but Herschel's mass of the sun, taking the mass of the earth as unity, is equal to 354,936 earths; resulting in the decrease of the weight of the sun by an amount nearly equal to 30,000 times the weight or gravity of the earth. By so much, at least, it is made to appear that the sun has not as much gravitating force by Newcomb's parallax as Herschel thought it had.

ENCKE'S SOLAR PARALLAX.

The American and English Nautical Almanacs

for 1864, accepted as an approximation to the
truth Encke's discussions of the transits of Venus
in 1761 and 1769, as furnishing the standard equatorial horizontal parallax of the sun at the earth's
mean distance=8".5776.   This parallax is equal
in linear measure to 3,841.671 miles.

HERSCHEL'S SOLAR PARALLAX.

Herschel, for just reasons, having objections
against the assumed integrity of Encke's solar parallax, makes the equatorial horizontal parallax of
the sun to equal 8".6, which in linear measure is
equal to 3,852 miles nearly.

NEWCOMB'S SOLAR PARALLAX.

Newcomb, departing from all former standards
and statements of the value of the solar parallax,
in his investigations of "the sun's distance," came
nearer to the goal of truth than any of his eminent
predecessors, and makes the equatorial horizontal
parallax of the sun to be 8".85, which in line
measure is equal to 3,963.657271 miles.

THE AUTHOR'S SOLAR PARALLAX.

My solar parallax of 8".8485, which is my cor-
rection of Newcomb's solar parallax, is in line
measure equal to 3,963 miles, and coincides with
the linear measure of the earth's equatorial radius.

The base line of every equatorial horizontal parallax, being the line of the earth's equatorial
radius=3,963 miles, the arc or angle of the parallax in degree should exactly equal a line measure
of 3,963 miles, and in any case when the line
measure of the arc or angle of the parallax is more
or less than 3,963 miles, the plus or minus is the
measure of the error involved.

TABLE OF SOLAR PARALLAXES IN ONE VIEW.

Encke's............8″.5776 is equal to 3,841.671 miles.
Herschel's...........8″.6 is equal to 3,852 miles.
Newcomb's........8″.85 is equal to 3,963.657271 miles.
The Author's.......8″.8485 is equal to 3,963 miles.

From the above it follows, that the line measure of the arc or angle of Encke's solar parallax is minus 121.329 miles, and that of Herschel's is minus 111 miles nearly, and the solar parallax of Newcomb's is plus .657271 fraction of a mile, requiring these corrections that each one of the parallaxes may equal 3,963 miles, with additions of corresponding degrees of angular measurements.

And if any mathematician or astronomer should be led, on further examination and discovery, to conclude that the line measure of the earth's equatorial radius should be taken to be less in measure than the term of 3,963 miles, which I have used in my work, the parallax should be correspondingly corrected, because mathematical law requires that the linear measure of the arc and tangent of any equatorial horizontal parallax should always coincide with the linear measure of the earth's equatorial radius, which is made the tangent of the angle.

In my determinations of the diameter and distance of the sun as they may be seen hereafter, I used the solar parallax of 8″.6, which I found in Herschel's *Outlines*, and in books of other learned authors, as being most consonant with the truth, which parallax I found, on subsequent examination, to be in error, by an amount in line measure of 111 miles nearly, and in angular measurement 0″.2485 of a degree.

My apology for not using my corrected equatorial horizontal parallax of the sun to the exclusion of that of 8″.6, by Herschel, is that Newcomb's work did not come into my possession until after all the subsequent part of my work was stereotyped.

KAISERLICHE AKADEMIE DER WISSENSCHAFTEN IN WEIN.

WEIN, den 26, *Marz*, 1868.

The Imperial Academy of Sciences, at Vienna, in the Empire of Austria (in a letter bearing the above caption and date), have tendered to me their thanks, and commanded their Secretary to convey to me their distinguished appreciation of my discoveries, and that they had deposited my works in their library. Then doing homage to genius, their letter concluded thus: "To the honored Sir WM. ISAACS LOOMIS, Pastor of the Piermont Baptist Church."

ASTRONOMICAL EPOCH OF MOSES,

Versus

Newton's System of the World and the American Bible Union.

A revised edition of the *Book of Genesis*, by Thomas J. Conant, on p. 4, speaks of a charge "against the sacred narrative, that it conflicts with the known truths of astronomy." According to Laplace and the tendency of the teaching of the Newtonian astronomers, the sun was caused to be before the earth, but Moses states the earth was caused to be on the first day, and the sun on the fourth day of the creation. What a difference! Because the structure of the planetary system of

Newton differs from that of Moses, all men should have, out of reverence for God the Creator, demanded a verdict against Newton ; but our poor erring eyesight, dazzled by the torchlight of the new science, clothed Newton with the honors of infallibility, and it was concluded that poor Moses, like an old fossil, should be laid on the shelf, to awaken our sympathy for the dark and ignorant age in which he lived.

A true interpretation of the facts of Natural Astronomy demonstrates that the motions of the earth are independent of any relation to the sun, and consequently the earth could have revolved in its orbit for seventy-two hours, or between three and four geologic ages, such as were guessed at by Agassiz and Hugh Miller, before the sun was caused to be.

Permit me now to say to the infidel Ha! ha!-ists who have concluded that they know more by the teachings of Newton than Moses ever learned of God : To the front, gentlemen, and learn that the narrative of Moses, in respect to the construction of the solar system, is in the most perfect accordance with Natural Astronomy.

WHAT MATHEMATICIANS HAVE PRONOUNCED MATHEMATICALLY IMPOSSIBLE, I HAVE DEMONSTRATED TO BE MATHEMATICALLY CERTAIN.

The science of Trigonometry teaches : In a triangle there are three sides and three angles, and that to limit the triangle to a particular form and size, three of the parts must be known, from which to determine the remaining three parts.

T. Dick, LL. D., affirms : "On the demonstrated

properties of a triangle depends the mode of measuring the distance of the sun and moon, the magnitudes of the planets, and the dimension of the solar system."

Here I join issue and affirm: That with two measures of the arc of the vertical angle of any one of the right-angled triangles projected in the equatorial horizontal parallaxes of the sun and planets, I can determine the linear measure of its perpendicular leg. Then the square root of the sum of the squares of the base and perpendicular leg will be the measure of the hypothenuse of the right-angled triangle, and the three sides will be determined. I hesitated not a little when I contemplated the disadvantages of my situation. On one side is congregated a galaxy of intelligences, formed of the mentally renowned of ages, composed of Atheists, Deists, Pagans, Roman Catholics, and Protestants, in one harmonious voice protesting against the success of my seemingly hopeless effort. On the other side, alone, and unsupported by the prestige of fame or ardent friends, a Baptist minister, coveting in this case to be crowned the mental king, engages to give a new lesson in science, that the living world of men will never forget.

First.—A star seen from the ends of the diameter of the earth's orbit exhibited an annual parallax of 1″ of a degree.

Second.—The triangle projected in the parallax is an isosceles triangle, and the line of bisection from the sun's centre to the star is the distance of the star from the sun's centre, the linear measure of which I will find.

Third.—The linear measure of the diameter of the earth's orbit, which arises from my corrected solar parallax, as before seen, is 184,760,833 miles.

Fourth.—The angle of the parallax being only one second of a degree, there can be no appreciable difference between the arc and tangent of the angle, and therefore the linear measure of the angle and arc of the parallax coincide.

The two measures of the arc of this parallax:

First.—The circular measure of the arc of 1″ of a degree carried to seven places of decimals is 0″.0000048, and is the divisor.

Second.—The linear measure of the arc is the same as that of the diameter of the earth's orbit, and is 184,760,833 miles, and is the dividend.

DEMONSTRATION BY DIVISION.

184,760,833,0000000÷48=38,490,840,000,000 miles, is the quotient, which is the distance of the star from the conditions of the example.

You have now the proof before you that the sublime problem of finding the distance of a star can be determined without any knowledge of trigonometry. Furthermore: in all equatorial horizontal parallaxes of the sun and planets, the arc of the parallax (which is the measure of the angle) IS AN ARC OF A CIRCLE, the *radius* of which is the required *mean distance* (see page 91), and all these examples can be solved, in fact are resolved in my work by common arithmetic, and hence you have the positive testimony, the most certain demonstration, that the bisecting line of an isosceles triangle, and the perpendicular leg of any right-angled triangle coming within the measures of angles of all the equatorial horizontal parallaxes can be determined without the use of trigonometry.

I have done what T. Dick declared to be impossible, and in my solutions of the diameters of the sun and planets by a simple proportion in common arithmetic, have invented a way in knowledge unknown to all the mathematicians who were before me ; and now I may be permitted to say : That though all the trigonometers are unanimous with Dick, the fact is brought to light that what they pronounced impossible I have demonstrated to be mathematically certain.

An Intellectual Excursion.

MEASURES OF THE CIRCLE.

1. MEASURE IN DEGREES.—The intelligent of mankind have concluded that 360° shall constitute the measure of the circle in degrees.

2. CIRCULAR MEASURE.—A circle whose radius is unity, the measure of its circumference, retaining seven places of decimals, is 6.2831853.

3. The circular measure of one second of a degree is 0.0000048, and any other measure between these can be found by proportion.

4. ARTIFICIAL MEASURE.—By dividing the circular measure of an arc of an angle, by the natural tangent of the angle, a quotient is obtained, which I have constituted the artificial measure of the arc.

How to find the perpendicular leg of a right-angled triangle when the angle of parallax is so large that the linear measure of its arc and tangent disagree. (See page 97.) In former cases, the linear measure of the arc was given, but when the linear measure of the arc of the angle is unknown, substitute for it the artificial measure of the arc of the angle, which may be found by dividing the circular measure of the arc of the angle, by the natural tangent of the arc of the angle, and the quotient will be the required term. Then by Proportion:—As the circular measure of the arc of the angle at the vertex : is to the artificial measure of the arc : : so is the base line of the right-angled triangle : to the linear measure of the required side.

THE HEIGHT OF A TOWER.

What is the height of a tower, if a line of 100 feet drawn from the bottom on a horizontal plane, subtends an angle of 42°30'? The circular measure of 42°30'=7417649 for the first term of a proportion, the artificial measure of 42°30'=80.94953 for the second term, and base line of the triangle 100 feet for the third term, and the fourth term will be the required height.

Demonstration.—As 7417649 : 80.94953 : : 100 feet : 109.13+feet, which is the height of the tower.

A like problem to find the height of a tower by Logarithms, may be seen in T. Dick's works, *Celestial Scenery*, page 143, which I will lay before the reader.

DICK'S PROBLEM.

Logarithm of the 2d term—Tangent of ....47½°==10.0379475
Logarithm of A B=100 feet—3d term....... 2.0000000

_____

12.0379475
Logarithm of radius—1st term.............. 10.0000000
Logarithm of C B, 4th term............==109⅛== 2.0379475

The answer 109.13 feet, by my method, is more exact than 109⅛ feet given by Dick. This exactness of result is the merit and glory of my discovery, the firm base on which it rests.

PROBLEM.—An observer at the mast-head of a

ship 66 feet high, looking at another ship, determines the angle of depression to be 10°. What is the distance of the two ships from each other?

Demonstration.—As the circular measure of 10°, which is 1745329 : is to the artificial measure of 10°, which is 98.98080 : : so is the height of the mast 66 feet : to 374.292 feet=22.68+rods.

Again my answer, 22.68+rods, is more exact than that given by Day and Thomson in a like problem, which is 22.66¾ rods.

If the height of an object is known, its distance may be known, by the circular and artificial measures of the arc of the angle of elevation, and the linear measure of its height.

PROBLEM.—A man on the bank of a river, from observations of a ship's mast, which is known to be 99 feet high, finds its angle of elevation to be 3°30′. What is the distance of the ship from the observer?

Demonstration.—As the circular measure of arc of 3½°, which is 0610865 : is to the artificial measure of arc of 3½°, which is 99.88636 : : so is 99 feet, the height of the ship's mast : to 1618.81 feet=98.1+rods, the required distance. Day and Thomson's Trigonometry, page 133, makes the answer 98 rods.

Practical Navigation. By N. Bowditch. Third Edition. Page 174.

BOWDITCH'S PROBLEM—VII.

Being 96 fathoms from the bottom of a tower, I found its altitude above the horizontal line drawn from my eye was 15°10′; required the elevation above that line?

Demonstration.—As the circular measure of arc

of 74°50′, which is 1.3060880 : is to the artificial
measure of arc of 74°50′, which is 35.40407 : : so
is 96 fathoms : to 26.023 fathoms. The answer
26.023 fathoms, by my method, is more exact, by
1.63 inch, than the answer 26 fathoms given by
Bowditch.

Required the height of Bunker Hill Monument,
if a line of 80.44 feet, measured from the bottom
on a horizontal plane, subtends an angle of 20°.

First.—Find the circular measure of the arc of
the given angle, which is obtained by the proportion :—As 360° : 20° : : 6.2831853 : 3490658 the
circular measure.

Second.—From a table of natural tangents select the natural tangent of the given angle, which
is 36379, and with it divide the circular measure
of the arc of the given angle, and the quotient will
be the artificial measure of the arc of the given
angle ; thus, 3490658÷36379=95.90510 which is
the artificial measure of an arc of 20°. Then by
proportion :—As 3490658 : 95.90510 : : 80.44
feet : 221.00 feet, the required height of the Monument.

The construction and use of tables of circular and
artificial measures of arc of 1″ and upward, and a
knowledge of a table of natural tangents, will un-
fold the science of right-angled triangles, in a
clearer light than ever known before.

The teachers of our common schools, after a
few hours' study, are prepared to adopt understandingly, my system of science, for finding the
sides of right-angled triangles, and all heights and
distances.

DISCOVERY

OF

THE ORIGIN OF GRAVITATION,

AND THE

MAJESTIC MOTIVE FORCE

WHICH

GENERATED THE DIURNAL AND YEARLY REVOLUTIONS

OF

THE HEAVENLY BODIES.

IN TWO PARTS.

BY

WILLIAM ISAACS LOOMIS,

Baptist Pastor.

MARTINDALE DEPOT, COLUMBIA CO., N. Y.

1866.

THOMAS HOLMAN,
Printer and Stereotyper.

To the Clergy.

In respect to the strangeness of my seeming assumptions, when compared with the believed certainty of the system of the world by Sir Isaac Newton, you may experience a shudder in consequence of my questioning the truth of a science which you have thought to be infallible, and grieve that a minister should be so unfortunate !

But if you will call to mind the wise men of the past, who were compelled from the force of facts to renounce long-cherished notions, you may then begin to think of the possibility of my having discovered the origin of gravitation and its sequences.

The position I have chosen is one of difficulty, and danger to the reputation of my wisdom. They crucified him, has been the lot of many, though they held in their hands the lamp of truth ! Asking for the sympathy of the holy, pure, and noble minded, I subscribe myself yours, in the hope of the ultimate triumph of the gospel of our Lord and Master, in the feast of love and reason, tempered by the love and intelligence of God.   WM. ISAACS LOOMIS.

To my Countrymen.

FINDING occasion to take exception to the accepted system of astronomy, I freely engage in the work.

In my investigations, I reached the conclusion that gravity is spheroidal and not universal ; and that nature requires but one motive force to produce the dual, or diurnal and yearly, motions of a heavenly body.

The Newtonian parallelogram of right-line forces, it will be seen, can not be resolved, other than imaginatively, into one force to cause the curvilinear motion of a globe.

The demonstration of this will arouse the learned world to an examination of the true right-line projectile and sidewise impulse, which is sufficient to cause the curvilinear motion observed in a heavenly body in its course round the sun.

In the sincere conviction that the time has come to begin a reformation in the Copernican system of astronomy, which is supposed to be founded in the immutable laws of nature, realizing the arduousness of the labor, and fearing the fate of my illustrious predecessors in innovation, I cross over the rubicon. Gladiators of science, to your posts, and like men of wisdom defend yourselves, if you can !

WM. ISAACS LOOMIS.

My Offering to my Nation.

———

An American consecrates this book of New Philosophy to the President of the United States of America and his Cabinet; to both Houses of Congress; to the Governors and Legislators of the States and Territories; to the Officers of the Army and Navy; to the Clergy, and other learned men; to every civilian, mother, sister, wife, and daughter; and I invoke your aid to help establish the new facts brought to light in this book.

With this offering, I breathe the prayer that our people may accomplish a national destiny that shall be glorious in the eyes of all men.

Yours in the hope of the nation,

WM. ISAACS LOOMIS.

PART FIRST.

בראשית

א

א בְּרֵאשִׁית בָּרָא אֱלֹהִים אֵת הַשָּׁמַיִם וְאֵת הָאָרֶץ:

TRANSLATION:

"God in the beginning created the heavens and the earth."—(Gen. i., 1.)

Commentary.

LET us conceive of the words heavens and earth to mean, in part, the moving worlds or globes of light which are to be seen in and from every part of the expanse ; and then we may contemplate the cause of the celestial motions, which, because of the adoption of false science, has been uncomprehended, until now for the first time revealed by an American.

Origin of Gravitation.

Sir Isaac Newton acted as grand master of ceremonies in introducing to mankind the knowledge of the law of universal gravitation, and he freely confessed his inability to discover the cause of it.

Since the demise of this most illustrious of mortals, the family of the scientific have been satisfied

with his doctrine of gravity; and, as far as I know,
I am the first to announce the knowledge of

The Discovery of the Origin of Gravitation.

To win the distinction incident to so great a discovery is a prize of more value than the gems and
fortunes of every earthly empire; for Fame stands
ready to crown the so distinguished king of the
mental realm.

The tempting honor and the hope of success in
this race for the mastery, and the faith that the
goal was in view, inspired me to say: I will try.
Is it not better to do and dare in a noble cause,
though failure blight the hopes, than ignobly to
fail in consequence of fear and indolence?

Universal Gravitation.

Universal gravitation is said to be a compara-
tive, reciprocal attraction of all particles of matter
among themselves, and that every particle of matter in the universe is attracted by every other
particle of matter, proportional to the densities and
distances of the particles from each other.

"What is Truth?"

Is the doctrine of universal gravitation true? Is
it a fact of nature? What are the known evidences
of its existence and operations? If it is true, and
a fact of nature, and operates to cause the periodic
revolutions of the heavenly bodies, the known testimonies of its existence are included in an inference. What! an inference! Yes. This is the
rock (?) on which was built the theory of the revolutions of celestial bodies. Because it appeared
that a law of gravity subjected the matter of the
earth and all bodies moving in the air to its sway,

Newton inferred that it might extend to the moon and all other bodies; and Newton, not nature, extended its empire, not knowing that the inference was drawn from spheroidal gravitation, the power of which does not extend beyond the atmosphere of the celestial body. I claim that, so far as the human mind is concerned in its possible comprehension of knowable objects, there is not in the amplitude of space even a solitary witness for the verity of the dogma of universal gravitation.

Should the curvilinear motions of the planets be cited as proof to the point, it can be demonstrated that the motion of a globe in the direction of a curve line in nowise depends on gravity.

Nature being without evidence to corroborate the splendid and so long serviceable inference, it comes under the ban of her empire; and however audacious the charge may seem to be to learned pedants and gentlemanly wise men, their zeal will be somewhat chastened when they reflect that all the evidence they can bring forth in defense of the law of universal gravitation is an inference. Could more have been done, Newton would have perfected the work. That he did no more, is a bar to all further inquiry in that direction.

Magnitudes.

In a time not long past, the orbit of Saturn was thought to be the outmost limit of the planetary boundary of the solar system. Then the magnitude of the sun was said to be five hundred times greater than all the magnitudes of all the other bodies belonging to the system of the sun.

Subsequent discoveries of the planet Uranus, with a real diameter of 33,570 miles, and the planet Neptune, with a real diameter of 33,392 miles, with their moons, and nearly one hundred asteroids, have greatly augmented the known weight of the satellites of the sun, while the weight of the sun has sensibly diminished.

Astronomical discoveries are climacteric, and further conquests in knowledge will bring to light other planets which revolve around the sun, in orbits beyond the orbit of Neptune, and a myriad of comets, besides a multitude of interplanetary asteroids, all of which, when aggregated and weighed against the sun, would have dragged the sun away from his central position, had the doctrine of universal gravity of matter, as taught by Newton, ever been true.

Diameters.

To our vision the apparent diameters of bodies become less in proportion as their distances are increased. If the sun's real diameter of 890,569 miles appears so small when viewed from the earth, what must be the dimensions of each star! The annual parallax and apparent diameters of the stars fall below one second of a degree ; but if, after the example of Herschel and others, we assume the stars to have an annual parallax, and also an apparent diameter of one second of a degree, the distance and real diameter may be determined, and the result will be that each star contains an amount of matter equal to about ten millions of suns. These things being premised, what is there, if the law of universal gravitation is true, to hinder the planet Neptune, at the time of his aphelion, from falling away from the sun toward the stars nearest his aphelion, the millions of which and their conjoined attractions constitute a force to attract Neptune which leaves that of the sun's attractive force wholly insignificant?

Lexicographical Disagreement.

That Webster and Worcester should disagree in their definitions of an annual parallax is startling. The base line of an annual parallax, according to Webster, is the diameter of the earth's orbit; the linear measure of which, according to my system of measurements of the solar system, is 190,099,404 miles. The base line of an annual parallax, according to Worcester, is the semi-diameter of the earth's orbit, the linear measure of which is 95,049,702 miles. Worcester's base line is that which was used by the astronomers in their trigonometrical solutions of annual parallaxes. Hence, in every case of solution of stellar parallax, the resulting distance has been but one half of what it should have been.

Webster's choice was natural, but that of Worcester was artificial. From Webster's base line and points of observations of an annual parallax of 1", the resulting distance is about forty trillions of miles; but from those of Worcester the resulting distance is about twenty trillions of miles.

Now, because Webster's base line is true to nature, and does arise in the observations incidental to an annual parallax, and does not mislead, like Worcester's is sure to do, being nothing more than an artificial creation, the artifice should be rejected, and that of Webster, on account of its integrity, should take its place in the true expositions of the celestial science.

Stellar Distances.

Let us assume that a star seen from the ends of the diameter of the earth's orbit would suffer an

apparent angular displacement of 1″ of a degree.
The angle so subtended is called the star's parallactic angle. Also seen from the star, the diameter
of the earth's orbit would subtend an angle of 1″
of a degree, which is called the angle of the parallax.

Instead of solving the example by trigonometry
and logarithms, I propose to do it by division,
using only the circular and linear measures of the
arc of the parallax.

RULE.

Use the circular measure of the arc of the parallax for a divisor, and the linear measure of the arc
of the parallax for a dividend, and the quotient
will be the required distance.

EXAMPLE.

Required the distance of a star, given the circular and linear measure of the arc of its annual
parallax of 1″ of a degree.

The circular measure of the arc of the parallax,
carried to seven places of decimals, is 0.0000048.

The linear measure of the arc of the parallax
equals the linear measure of the diameter of the
orbit of the earth, and is 190,099,404 miles.

Demonstration. — 190,099,404.0000000 miles÷
48=39,604,042,500,000 miles,=the star's distance
from the centre of the sun.

Real Diameter of a Star.

In nature, the parallax of a heavenly body, its
apparent diameter, the base line of the parallax,
and the real diameter, are in a geometrical ratio;
from which I have derived the following rule,
which may be resolved by common arithmetic.

RULE.

As the parallax of any body on the surface of the earth, or celestial body, is to its apparent diameter, so is the base line of the parallax to a fourth term, which will be the real diameter.

EXAMPLE.

Given the annual parallax, apparent diameter, and base line, to find the real diameter by common arithmetic.

Demonstration.—As the star's annual parallax of 1″ is to the star's apparent diameter of 1″, so is the base line of the parallax of 190,099,404 miles to 190,099,404 miles, which is the star's real diameter.

In the use of my two rules, all examples in respect to finding distances and diameters may be resolved, and the royal road to the solutions of the sublime examples afforded by astronomy is thrown open to all who understand common arithmetic. I am aware of the objections which may be urged in opposition to my views on this point: that there is not a star but has a less amount of parallax and apparent diameter than those I have mentioned. I accept the objection, because it makes in my favor; for if you reduce the parallax and apparent diameter, the star's distance is correspondingly increased, and its real diameter augmented. What I wished to do, was to find the least distance within which there is not a star, and, gaining an approximate or least probable size of a star, bring the vast bulks of the star-worlds to bear on the subject of universal gravitation, and I am assured that the learned will find no just cause of objection against the hypothesis.

Neptune's Opposition.

At the time of an opposition of the planet Neptune, I determined his distance from the sun to be 2,850,115,900 miles.

Being prepared with the necessary magnitudes and distances, we may now represent the distance of Neptune from the sun by unity, or 1. Then the distance of Neptune from the sun will be to Neptune's distance from the stars as 1 to 13,895; and estimating the bulk of the sun as unity, and comparing the bulk of the sun with the bulk of a star, the sun will be to the star as 1 to about 10,000,000. What if the matter composing the sun is five hundred times greater than that of all the bodies of his system? The matter of a single star is millions of times greater than that of the sun; and this enormous mass, conjoined with millions of like bodies, should, if the accepted theory is true, compel Neptune to increase his distance from the sun and lessen his distance from the stars. But this is not the case, and never can be; and the absence of such an active force can not be explained away by the apology of the vast distance.

Gravity, to be universal, must act. And if under any circumstances it does not, what next follows, but that gravity is not universal and stands impeached?

Contemplate the planet Neptune, in the pomp of his yearly journey, moving round the sun. At the point of his aphelion, not only one, but millions of stars nearer to him than others on the opposite side of the planet toward the sun reach forth their long arms of gravitation, if they have any, to embrace this outside world. But no. Neptune, true to the one right-line projectile force which gave birth to his motions, and owning fealty to no other, pursues his continuous journey without being in the least disturbed by any other force.

For a moment consider gravity under the figure of weight. The weight of the matter of the sun is to the weight of the matter of a star as 1 to 10,000,000. Multiply this large figure by the many millions of stars nearest to Neptune, to represent the weight of the stellar matter to be opposed to the weight of the sun against Neptune. Then the square of the distances considered, the weight of the sun against Neptune, compared with the weight of the stars against Neptune, will cause the weight of the sun to appear lighter than the fine dust of the balance, and of no moment in the inquiry, What causes the curvilinear motion of the planet Neptune?

Comets.

H. Westphalen, in his *Elements of Halley's Comet*, assigns 3,370,300,000 miles as the greatest distance of the comet from the sun. This is more than five hundred and twenty millions of miles further from the sun than is the aphelion point of Neptune's orbit.

Consequently, Halley's Comet, when at his aphelion, is most favorably situated to be brought under the attractions of the stars nearest to the aphelion point; but such attractions, if they exist, live only in inference. While the possibility of a body falling into the sun in consequence of his attraction has been assumed, none of the sons of science have ever been exercised with the fear of the bodies of the system of the sun falling away outward as an effect of the gravity of the stars. The force that originated the curvilinear motion of this comet, and the regularity of its periodic revolution, forbid the possibility of such a deflection ever taking place.

COMET OF 1811.

The comet of 1811 requires three thousand years, measured as we measure years on the earth, to complete its year of revolution round the sun, and when at its aphelion point its distance from the sun is 160,000,000,000 of miles.

The aphelion distance of this comet being made unity, or 1, if it is compared with my stellar distance, bears the proportion of 1 to 247 ; or if compared with the astronomers' distance of the stars, is as 1 to 123 +, exhibiting a very near approach to the stars. Were the doctrine of the gravitation of the celestial orbs among themselves consonant with nature, this comet must obey the superior attraction, and launch away into the depths of the wilderness of stars, and revolve around stellar orbs, whose magnitudes are the exposition of God's almightiness. But there being no mutual attractions of orbs among themselves, or exterior to the atmospheres of the heavenly bodies, they are left free to obey the force which once having marked their ways, they follow in those paths continually.

COMETS OF 1680 AND 1843.

The perihelion, or nearest distance to the sun, of the comet of 1680 was only 148,428 miles.

The perihelion, or nearest distance to the sun, of the comet of 1843 was only 63,613 miles.

Let the reader suppose that the force of what is called the gravity of the sun is exerted on the comets of 1680 and 1843 at the instant they attained their aphelion points, and that the Newtonian centripetal and centrifugal forces at those times are equally adjusted to each other. The centrifugal force must remain constant; but the centripetal force, as the comets move from their greatest to their least distances from the sun, will increase as the square of the distances decrease. Therefore, when the comets have reached their nearest distances from the sun, the centripetal force being so overwhelmingly increased, and the centrifugal or projectile force being the same constant quantity at either equinox or solstice of these cometary orbits, what is there to prevent these comets rushing to the body of the sun? But they do not. Is it because they are such anomalous bodies, or is there something more to be known before we have the grand secret of curvilinear motion?

A Concession.

The difficulties of my situation are relieved not a little by concessions of the very learned in this science, that there have been observed phenomena which can not be accounted for by the law of universal gravitation, nor can the accepted laws of motion be relied on to explain the lawless appearances. Pertinent are the examples of the tails of the comets of 1680 and 1843, as they were known to move round the sun, "in the manner of a straight and rigid rod, in defiance of the law of gravitation, nay, even of the received laws of motion." (See Herschel's *Outlines*, p. 323.)

The lamented Mitchel, whose beautiful grace of diction suffers no loss when contrasted with the grand pomp of T. Dick's style, says of the tail and nucleus of a comet: " 4. That the force which ejects the tail can not be gravitation. 5. That the power lodged in the nucleus, and by whose energy the particles composing the tail are again

reabsorbed into the head, can not be gravitation."
(See O. M. Mitchel's *Popular Astronomy*, p. 298.)

Does it now look as if the day-spring of hope and
truth had burst in upon our expectations? As if
the morning star in its glow of promise preluded a
day of glory in which humanity, in communion with
nature, might learn how God worked, and by what
agency? Have we not reached a point where
the concessions of Herschel and Mitchel strip the
law of universal gravitation of some part of its
empire? If some of the heavenly bodies disdain
to move round the sun, as an effect of gravitation
and the received laws of motions, why may not all
bodies be equally independent? It is a favorite
notion with those who have dealt in celestial
mechanics that the reciprocal gravity of the
matter of the celestial spheres among themselves
is greater at less distances, less at greater distances,
and that every particle of matter is subject to this
law.

Take it for Granted.

When the earth is at the aphelion point of its
orbit, its distance from the sun, is (3,000,000) three
millions of miles greater, than when at its perihelion or least distance; consequently, every pound
of matter of and on the earth should weigh more
at the earth's least distance, and less at the greatest
distance. But a succession of the changes of
weight, incidental to the sun's attraction, is unknown among men.

ILLUSTRATION.

Assume that somewhere on the equator there
is located a spiral spring balance, which in its very
nature could not be sensibly affected by the force

of universal gravitation, and capable of weighing the steamship Great Eastern. With the ship hanging or resting on the balance, its weight, being determined at any point, would be in a continual change, as the earth in the course of its yearly journey moved round the sun; and this mutation would also be true of the matter of all other heavenly bodies, if the sun's attraction held the empire with which Newton endowed it. But the constancy of weight of the matter of the earth, and all that pertains to it, whether the earth is at its least, greatest, or intermediate distances from the sun, is proof conclusive that the square of the distance has nothing to do in respect to all earthly things.

Do you Believe it?

The gravity of the earth being exclusively spheroidal, having more than an inferential existence, can be demonstrated to the perception of the inquirer, and its activity be determined. Again call to mind the steamship on the equator, as before mentioned, with its weight determined at the present rate of the motion of the earth on its axis. Now, because spheroidal attraction exists, every change in the time of the earth's rotation would be accompanied with a change, not only of the weight of the Great Eastern, but also of the whole matter of the earth. If the centrifugal force of the earth should be diminished, the weight of the ship would be correspondingly increased, and any change of the time of the axial rotation would cause a change of the weight of the matter of the earth and everything in relation to it. The reason why we can demonstrate the change of weights, from spheroidal gravitation incident to a change in the time of rotary motion, is placed beside the inoperative law of universal gravitation, and the reader is requested to closely examine into the nature of things.

The Matter of the Universe.

REASONINGS IN PHILOSOPHY.

I.

The matter of the universe when in a state of rest was without any kind of attraction or tendency to any centre, and its weight was absolute.

II.

When the matter of the universe was passed from a state of rest to a state of motion round the axes of the oblate spheroids which compose the family of the heavenly bodies, the matter of each oblate sphere tended to its axial centre, and, being opposed by the centrifugal force of the body, pressed less heavily than it otherwise would have done if the centrifugal force had been less, and therefore the weight of the matter of a moving oblate spheroid is less than its absolute weight.

III.

The gravity or tendency of the matter of a moving oblate spheroid is determined by the amount of centrifugal force generated by the rotary motion of the sphere, and the gravity is increased or diminished in proportion as you may find the rotary motion diminished or increased from a given standard, so that the measure of the force of the gravity of a heavenly body is a creature of circumstances.

IV.

The tendency of the matter of a sphere to its axial centre, which is the force of its attraction of gravitation, was originated coeval with the force that generated the rotary motion of the sphere. Now if the matter of the sun was solid gold, and his centrifugal force was increased to equal the absolute weight of the gold, the weight of the sun would be thrown into a state of equilibrium, not tending to his centre, and without gravity. Now reduce the force of the rotary motion, which will reduce the centrifugal force, and instantly the mass of the matter of the sun will tend to his axial centre, and this attraction of gravitation may be increased more and more, as the rotary motion of the sun is reduced less and less, rendering certain what I before said: That the attraction of the gravity of a sphere is a creature wholly of circumstances.

V.

To suppose that matter, in its very nature, is necessarily endowed with the mysterious power of universal gravitation, is to assume that matter is endowed with power to move, and does move itself by its own inhering power, which is contrary to nature; and in doing so, Newton on the attraction of gravitation is contradicted by Newton on the impossibility of matter to move itself.

VI.

A WONDER.

Four resulting motions generated by a single right-line force.

The phenomena of the four resulting motions known to belong to a moving oblate sphere arose from a single right-line sidewise projectile force which changed the state of its matter from rest to motion. They are:

1. The forward curvilinear motion of the sphere.

2. The rotary motion of the sphere.

3. The centrifugal motion of the sphere.

4. The centripetal motion, or the tendency of the matter of the sphere to its axial centre.

These four motions and their forces were the offspring of one right-line force, and they were simultaneously started into being.

The novelty of their begetting, the certainty of their relation, their antiquity, and hitherto unknown origin, constitute one of those beautiful revelations of truth so well calculated to advance knowledge.

The Natural Law of Gravitation.

Right or wrong, it is a bold endeavor to attempt to point out the way of light and truth, on a subject in which the colossus of intelligence was immersed in densest darkness. Newton (in his *Principia*, p. 506 of Book 111,) says: "But hitherto I have not been able to discover the cause of those properties of gravity from phenomena." The mere thought that I am able to demonstrate what gravity is, and how it was originated, is as refreshing as the odors of Paradise, and all-animating as the attainment of the utmost bound of earthly hope.

It is so in Nature.

The natural law of gravity is spheroidal and not universal, and it is the tendency of the matter of a moving oblate sphere to its axial centre, and was generated by the force which gave rise to the rotary motion of the sphere. Without the action of the rotary motion of the sphere its gravity ceases to be, and matter then could be contemplated only in a state of absolute rest. This tendency of the matter of a sphere to the centre of its axial motion I call the centripetal force of the sphere, and it is to be distinguished from what Newton calls the centripetal force to urge all the matter of the globe to its centre; and also that centripetal force of the sun, which Newton thought compelled the celestial bodies to move in the direction of curve lines.

Therefore, the gravity or centripetal force of the sun is the tendency of the matter of the sun to his axial centre. Opposed by the sun's centrifugal force, his weight will be relatively less than his absolute weight, and the force of this relative weight will be the measure of the force of the gravity of the sun. The same is true of every oblate moving sphere in the universe, be it a planet, satellite, asteroid, comet, or star; and any other kind of gravitation is unknown in the creation, and not necessary to account for any celestial phenomena.

Inferences.

1. If any celestial body is seen or known to have an axial rotation, it must be an oblate spheroid.

2. If any celestial body is seen or known to move in the direction of a curve line, it must have an axial rotation also; and from the phenomenon of the curvilinear motion, the axial motion may be inferred, and also the oblate form may be inferred without further observations; for in nature, a body moving in free space, its before-mentioned motions and form are inseparable from each other, being works of nature, from the order and relation of which there is never a departure.

The Origin of Spheroidal Gravitation.

It is a truth to be admitted, and certainly without the fear or possibility of believing error, that in the creation of matter it was not endowed with power to move itself.

The God of nature having gathered the matter of the celestial orbs, and assigned to each one its quantity and variety, each celestial body, by a single motive sidewise force, was urged into four distinct motions, one of which was the tendency of the matter of the sphere to its axial centre. Now because this tendency of the matter of a celestial orb to its centre is the centripetal force, or gravity of the matter of the orb, and there being no other demonstrable kind of gravity of attraction, we find the origin of the gravitation of each one of the celestial bodies in the right-line forces which caused the motions of every celestial body. Hence the motive force which caused the motions of the earth generated the gravity of the earth.

EXPERIMENT.

Experiment in which it will be shown that a given quantity of matter may be withdrawn from the gravity of the earth and brought under another force of gravity.

Suppose a truly spherical globe, twenty-four inches in diameter, held by some adequate means in a relative state of rest; at a distance of five feet from the surface of the earth, ready to have communicated to it a motion on an axis parallel with the horizon.

A globe so suspended is an example of a certain amount of matter withheld from the visible attraction of spheroidal gravitation.

If the globe should be disengaged it would fall to the earth; or if immediately under it there was an ordinary well, or shaft, or deepest artesian well of capacity to admit the globe, it would find its way to the deepest unobstructed point. The globe, in its descent, is a visible example of matter subjected to the attraction of spheroidal gravitation.

Let us now pour on the globe, as before supposed, above the surface of the earth and relatively at rest, a quantity of liquid, which, being free to flow, diffuses itself over the surface of the globe, and from the underside is seen to trickle to the earth; if the solid globe could be resolved gradually into a fluid mass, drop by drop it also would fall to the earth, being entirely subjected to the attraction of spheroidal gravitation.

The Change.

But the case will be substantially changed, notwithstanding the globe is within the atmosphere of the earth, and subject to the force of its gravity; for if you communicate to the globe a rotary motion, the matter of the globe will be withdrawn from the attraction of the earth, and tend to the centre of the globe. This new force of gravity was generated with the axial motion of the globe.

Now pour on the revolving globe a small quantity of water, which being arrested by the force of the axial rotation, the water and the entire matter of the globe seek and tend to its axial centre. This tendency of the matter of the revolving globe and the water revolving on its surface is an example of the existence of spheroidal gravitation. Now mark! When the globe was supposed at rest, its matter and the water poured on it tended to gravitate to the earth; but as soon as the globe had communicated to it a rotary motion, its matter tended to gravitate to its centre, and its proximity to the earth in no degree interfered with this new direction of the gravity of the matter of the globe. The same must be true of a larger quantity of denser matter poured on the rotating globe, such as molasses or tar, which, diffusing itself over

the surface of the globe, will gather thickest at its
equator, thus changing the form of the globe into
that of an oblate spheroid.

This, in a small but effective degree, shows how
matter may be arrested and gather round a centre
of centripetal force, and why the matter of a rotating globe is restricted to the form of an oblate
sphere.

Difficulties in Human Theories.

The dogma of universal gravitation involves the
idea that every heavenly body is continually falling
toward every other heavenly body.

To prevent the bodies colliding in a grand catas-
trophe, a right-line motive projectile force was
invented, and the attracting force of the sun, conjoined with the planets' projectile force, simultaneously drawing and driving every heavenly body in
right lines perpendicular to each other, constitutes
a confusion of motions that could be thought to be
reasonable only by men who allowed their reason to
be prostrated in devotion to the false second law of
motion.   In the words of a celebrated astronomer :
"In one sense, the moon is continually falling to the
earth."   And so must the moon and earth be continually falling to the sun, and the sun be continually falling to both earth and moon.   The moons
of Jupiter are continually falling to their primary,
and both Jupiter and his moons are continually
falling to the sun ; and the sun continually falling to
Jupiter and his moons.   In fact, according to the
received theory, every satellite of the solar system
is falling to the sun, and the sun is falling toward
every other celestial body of the solar system.
This, if true, is truly a grand contortion of nature ;
a universal and perpetual tumbling.   If you please,

you will now suppose with La Place and Pontecou-
lent, that originally the centripetal force of matter
gathered a nebulous mass out of which to form
the solar system, and that the axial rotation of this
mass generated a centrifugal force which was
competent to throw off into space, from time to
time, first a mass to constitute the planet Neptune
and his moons, and successively every other celestial body of the system. As the mass of matter
subsequently to be known as the planet Neptune
and his moons was hurled forth into space, it
must, according to the received first law of motion,
have moved forward in the direction of a right
line. When it had reached its greatest distance in
that line, how, or by what means, was a projectile
force, at that instant, ready to impinge on the
mass and urge it in the direction of a line perpendicular to the line in which it had moved in the
interval from the time of the separation to that of
its greatest distance from the centre of the original
mass? The question involves a difficulty that true
astronomy never could or would involve, fatal
alike to the La Placean origin of the celestial
spheres, and the dogma of universal gravitation.

It is particularly worthy of notice, that, in the
La Placean origin of the universe, at the instant
when the mass of matter to be afterward known
as the planet Neptune and his moons was ready
to be separated from the great body of matter,
in consequence of the centrifugal force of the mass,
all attraction between the mass to be separated
and that that remained was not only overcome,
but more than that, by an amount of force equal
to the centrifugal force which launched the mass
into space.

If, then, at that time the attraction of the matter of the whole solar system was more than
overcome by centrifugal force, and the mass of
Neptune could be no longer held by it, and the attraction growing less and less every instant as the
square of the distance increased, how absurd even
to think of the mere possibility, much less to state
it as science, that when Neptune was within one
inch of the surface of all the matter of the solar
system, himself alone excepted, and under the
whole force of the attraction of the whole solar
system, he escaped from it, and fled away to a
distance of 2,850,115,900 miles, but was there
arrested by the attraction of the sun which now
controls Neptune's orbital motion; the sun, by its
attraction alone, now doing what the whole solar
system could not do by its whole attractive force
when Neptune's proximity to the surface of the
whole mass was less than one hundred barley-
corns!   Who can believe it?

PART SECOND.

—◆—

Treatise on Motions.

IN WHICH IT IS ESTABLISHED THAT THE RESULTING MOTIONS WHICH INHERE IN EACH HEAVENLY BODY WERE GENERATED BY A RIGHT-LINE SIDEWISE FORCE.

A LAUDABLE ambition to obtain a knowledge of nature will ennoble men, and in every sense better qualify a child of God to enjoy communion with his Maker. The High and Holy One, who inhabits eternity, has made the earth man's birth and burial place. In it he blooms like a flower, and fades away like a leaf. Now on God's footstool confessing his sins and asking for pardon through the crucified Redeemer, and then ready to pass through the porch of death, on his way to immortality, to the house of God, and the home of the holy. There and then all the sanctified in Jesus will have learned the science of nature, and say in glorious acclaim: Great and marvelous are thy works, Lord God Almighty!

How many godlike intelligences,—endowed by their Creator with capability, if put forth, to stand in the first rank with heroes in mind, and lead the way in developing facts of nature,—content themselves in providing food for the stomach, nerves, and blood, but leave the mind to wander in indescribable darkness, having no better understanding of the celestial motions than usually falls to the lot

of the colt of a wild ass. And what is the number
of ministers and Christians who might, if they
would try, be able to grasp the solar and sidereal
spheres, but choose to content themselves with ig-
noring the works of God in nature, as a kind of
second-hand affair, unworthy of a Christian's devotional notice, and go to their graves indifferent to
the grandeur of their heavenly Father's empire.
Strangers to that vast field of vision, in which he
designs to show the triumph of his redeeming and
eternal love.

An advance in all attainable knowledge should
be determined by every one, and to know for
thyself is the acme of the feast of reason; for that
which is known to be true, by the evidence of demonstration to the reasoning powers of the human
mind, can never be other than true.

Had the followers of Aristotle required of their
teacher one reason, or had one of his disciples tried
an experiment to elucidate the law of falling
bodies, as Galileo did at the Leaning Tower of
Pisa, to find a reason for the science, it is reasonable to conclude the true law of falling bodies had
been known earlier, and Galileo would not have
had the opportunity to discover and lay a stone
in the foundation of a philosophy on which Sir
Isaac Newton built his system of the world.

Instead of assuming and then laboring to convert
the assumptions into facts, had Ptolemy detected
the dual motion of the apparent diurnal and yearly
sun, which he saw but did not perceive, the vision
of so stupendous a glory of God in nature would
have compelled Ptolemy to give an everlasting
good-by to his and also to his illustrious predecessors' fanciful notion of a fixed earth and really

moving sun. Could Ptolemy have traced the solar motions to their causes, his system of the world, which was but the echo of a false theory, would be in the deep quiet of the unknown.

But look at Ptolemy, as he thinks he sees the sun in real motion and stands on the firm earth. His eyesight is not impaired, his sense of the immobility of the earth undoubted; but an appeal to nature changes one of the most celebrated philosophers of antiquity into an erring blind man, who had never truly seen the beauties, and without an understanding of the appearances of nature. Ptolemy is an illustrious example of the truth of my apothegm, that in this world there is not anything so much like a lie as the truth; and this is the reason why, not only Bible truth, but also the truth of the science of astronomy has been so poorly understood.

The fact of man's success in discoveries in the science and causes of things depends on how much God's inspiration is breathed on the toiling one; but those who, like Hugh Miller, lean too much to their own understanding will, like him, stumble into positive failures.

That great geologist, having neglected all idea of deriving help from any other source than what his abstract observations resulted in, found it easy in this isolation to worm himself out of the way marked out by infinite wisdom.

The man who could find in a fragment of stone, or ledge of rocks, or fossil remains, evidence for believing in their creation and being millions of years before the Adamic epoch, had the ability to convert multitudes to the wonders of his scheme; and when he brought forth the fossil dung that

was found among the treasuries of nature, having
been carefully preserved in her archives for millions of years, it proved to be the natural archi-
episcopal rite of confirmation to all his followers.
After this, there remained but little to do in the
way of demonstrating whatever might be required
to make firm and establish the geological scheme.

But one thing more was wanted to establish this
anti and ante Mosaic chronology of the creation,
and that was a deluge in a respectable-sized " basin."   Mr. H. Miller clearly understood that a universal deluge, like that described by Moses, seen
and experienced by Noah, and testified of by a
bosom friend of the Savior, " The world that then
was, being overflowed with water, perished," must
not be admitted, or else Hugh Miller's geology,
which he thought had grown hoary in the lapse
of millions of millions of years, must fail for want of
testimony.   This one thing was supplied, and the
awe-inspiring Bible narrative of the Deluge was
transmogrified into a partial deluge, about as necessary for the purpose as a deluge in a wash-tub !

Had the Deluge been in a " basin," there had
been no need for the ark and the congregating of
the creatures.   They and Noah and his family
could easily have journeyed beyond its limits, and
it would have sufficed for God to have said to
Noah and his family, to the creatures of every
kind, as was said to Lot: "Arise, and get thee
out of this place, for I will destroy it."   This idea
of a partial deluge, of so celebrated a geologist, is
the most sublime approach to a tempest in a tea-
pot of anything yet brought forth by the grand
masters of science, and still there remains room for
the wise to learn.

False Science—A Concatenation of Mistakes.

MISTAKE OF PTOLEMY.

Ptolemy assumed the earth to be fixed, and the sun to really move around it.

Take a terrestrial globe to represent the fixed earth of Ptolemaic conception, and mark upon it circles to represent the circles of the ecliptic and equinoctial ; procure also two lamps, to represent the apparent motions of the sun. Pass one of the lamps round the globe, following the circle which represents the circle of the ecliptic, and let this motion of the lamp represent the motion of the apparent sun of nature describing the circle of the ecliptic. Then pass the second lamp round the circle of the globe which represents the circle of the equinoctial, and let this motion of the lamp represent the apparent diurnal sun of nature, as he is seen nearly describing the great circle of the equinoctial on the day of the vernal or autumnal equinox.

Hence it is plainly to be seen, that if the earth had been a fixed body one really moving sun could not have produced the phenomena of the solar motions of nature. The testimony of the solar motions, understood, dissolves every shadow of reason in support of a fixed earth ; but the wonder remains : How could the wise of this world, for so many generations, remain in darkness, and permit their eyesight and common-sense to be so long perverted by the blinders of the Ptolemaic fixed earth ?

MITCHEL'S MISTAKE.

In the system of Ptolemy the sun was said to have but one kind of motion ; but in the verities of nature the sun has two kinds of apparent motion. In the presence of such a tangible distinction and palpable fact, it is one of the strange things that have happened that philosophers, men of glorious eminence, who had the bright beams of the sun to guide them to the fountain of truth, should have so signally failed to find the clear way.

It was no fault of nature that occasioned the hiding of the truth, no obscurity that vailed the subject, for God had written the lesson in sunlight on the heavens; but a defect in the education of those students of nature, that led them astray.

So the men who see in our Jesus no form of winning loveliness should drop their unbelief, and see the light of his glory. It shines! No excuse for you that you have not seen it. Look to the Sun of our righteousness through the tears of sins confessed! Behold the solar motions of his love and pity for you! As you look you will rejoice, and say: I behold the Lamb in his glory, as unconverted eyes never yet beheld him.

In O. M. Mitchel's *Popular Astronomy*, pp. 63 and 64: "If, then, we confine our attention principally to an examination of the solar and lunar motions, in our efforts to determine the true position and condition of the earth, we shall find ourselves compelled, as were the celebrated Greek astronomers, Hipparchus and Ptolemy, to admit not only the earth's central position, but also its absolute immobility. It is, undoubtedly, central to the moon's motions, and it is equally central to the sun's movements; that is to say, all the phenomena of the solar motions are as well accounted for by supposing the earth to be the centre about which the sun revolves, as by supposing the converse hypothesis, that the sun is the centre about which the earth revolves. So far, then, as these two great luminaries are concerned, the hypothesis of the earth's central position is well sustained and almost indisputable." The celebrity of Mitchel should have made him proof against the attempt to pass this communication off for truth, or anything like that found in his remarks which I have laid before the reader. What is there in nature that sustains indisputably, in any degree, "the earth's central position?" To the barbarian, the unlettered son of civilization, and erring astronomers, the earth may seem to occupy a central position; but these seemings of ignorance of those in error should not be put even in the likeness of the truth, compared with which there is no resemblance; and hence Mitchel, in deciding that the two-fold or dual appearing diurnal and yearly solar motions are the same, whether seen from a fixed Ptolemaic earth and a real moving sun, or from a really moving earth and fixed sun, erred so widely as to justly excite astonishment.

WHEWELL'S MISTAKE.

William Whewell (in his *History of the Inductive Sciences*, Vol. I., pp. 257 and 258,) says: "For is it in reality clear, that before the time of Copernicus the heliocentric theory (that which places the centre of the celestial motions in the sun) had a claim to assent so decidedly superior to the geocentric theory, which places the earth in the centre? What is the basis of the heliocentric theory? That the relative motions are the same on that and on the other supposition. So far, therefore, the two hypotheses are exactly on the same footing. But, it is urged, on the heliocentric side we have the advantage of simplicity. True; but we have on the other side the testimony of our senses; that is, the geocentric doctrine (which asserts that the earth rests and the heavenly bodies move) is the obvious and spontaneous interpretation of the appearances."

Review the language and logic of Whewell's statement. Masterly and beautiful in composition, but false in principle. He decides that the dual motions of the apparent sun of nature are identical with the one motion of a real sun moving round a fixed earth.

If in this case Mitchel and Whewell have given us a fair specimen of the accuracy of the Copernican system of astronomy, its reliableness may be justly called in question, and its stability quivers already in approaching impeachment.

When Whewell affirms, "we have the testimony of our senses that the real sun moves round an imaginary fixed earth," that this "is the obvious and spontaneous interpretation of the appearances," did he mean our senses perverted by ignorance and false science, or our correctly educated senses? Which?

It is so, to our perverted senses the sun seems to go round the earth; but when our educated senses are put in communion with the verities of nature, the illusion vanishes. It is not supposable that Whewell meant that to our perverted senses the sun moves around a fixed earth in one motion, and that this is the obvious and spontaneous interpretation of the solar motions. His intelligence forbids this assumption, for every educated person knows, senses, and distinguishes the apparent motions of the sun. What, then, was meant? We

are driven to the conclusion that a great mistake
has been made, rendered not the less so by the
great names engaged in it, and that the understood
true solar motions are in no wise identical with the
phenomenon of the real motion of one sun. The
principal source of all error has been the perver-
sion of the senses of mankind by false teaching,
equally damaging in science and religion. A false
science perverted the senses of Hipparchus and
Ptolemy. Hence they wittingly thought they saw
what was not to be seen in the appearances of
nature. The same want of a true perception, and
the adoption of theory for truth, has kept mankind
so long in the darkness of scientific error, and from
the taint of this original corruption Wm. Whewell
did not escape.

BRADLEY'S MISTAKE.

Bradley's discovery of the annual aberration of
the light of the stars was hailed as positive evidence of the earth's annual motion; but because
the stars which are seen in the plane of the celestial equator at the time of the summer solstice are
also seen in the plane of the celestial equator at
the time of the winter solstice, nature afforded no
opportunity for Bradley's pseudo discovery.

The stars appear and are known to change their
place, with respect to an earthly observer, in every
instant of time during the earth's diurnal revolution; and therefore nature does afford an opportunity to make the discovery of the diurnal aberration of the light of the stars, which was made after
Bradley's death.

Bradley, no doubt, discovered the diurnal aberration of the light of the stars, which he mistook
for their annual aberration; and since his day the

mistake has been lauded as a fact of nature, and afforded to astronomers a wonderful field in which to display their erudition in fanciful astronomy, in assuming what would be if Bradley's discovery had been verity, and not a myth as it is.

FOR ASTRONOMERS.

MY DEMONSTRATION OF THE EARTH'S MOTIONS.

Law of Nature.

In the fact of a planet simultaneously turning on an axis and moving round a central sun, the dual motion of the planet will be transferred to the sun, causing the sun in appearance to have a dual motion, resulting in apparent diurnal and yearly revolutions of the central sun ; and from the solar motions observed from any one of the heavenly bodies may be deduced the nature of the motions of the heavenly globe. Now, because the phenomena of the solar motions observed from the earth are diurnal and yearly, from these apparent motions I deduce the facts of the diurnal and yearly motions of the earth, without any respect to the changes of the seasons, or Bradley's discovery of the annual aberration of the light of the stars. In so doing I am conscious that not a known astronomer of the past has ever attempted to demonstrate the earth's annual motion as I have done.

The Copernican-Newtonian astronomers give, in proof of the earth's annual motion, the changes of the seasons; but if, as Mitchel and Whewell say, "whether of the earth around the sun or of the sun around the earth," the appearances of nature are the same, the testimony of the changes of the seasons is of but little force ; but if you regard as forcible and true the deducing of the earth's axial and orbital motions from the apparent motions of the sun, then the testimony of the four seasons of

the year greatly add to the testimony of the solar
motions, and these proofs or testimonies of nature
to the wise are convincing.

What is to be Seen.

At the time of the vernal equinox, if an observer
in the position of a right sphere draws a line passing through the centres of the earth and sun, produced to the stars, and with this line draws a circle,
the circle will be the circle of the ecliptic among the
stars, and the space cut by the line will be the plane
of the ecliptic. With another line drawn from the
centre of the earth, passing through the line of the
equator, produced to the stars, describe a circle,
which will be the circle of the celestial equator;
and the circles of the ecliptic and equator are inclined to each other about 23° 28′.

At the instant of the beginning of the astronomical year, the centre of the apparent sun being on
the point of intersection of the planes of the
ecliptic and equinoctial, an observer, under the
effects of the dual motions of the earth, will see the
centre of the sun in appearance move in the plane
of the ecliptic, and also in the plane of the equinoctial. As an effect of the diurnal motion of the
earth, the diurnal sun will finish a solar day revolution; and as an effect of the yearly motion of
the earth round the sun, the sun will appear to
complete a solar year revolution.

A Wonder of Creation.

One of God's great works in the creation was
his making a real sun answer the purposes of a
multitude of apparent suns. If we had the power
to multiply our personal being to equal the number of the bodies of the solar system, and could

take a position on every one of them in the same instant, the apparent sun would be seen describing a multitude of diurnal revolutions in the several times of the diurnal revolutions of all the celestial bodies; and observed from each one of the heavenly bodies, the apparent sun would be seen describing a multitude of yearly revolutions equal in number to the number of the bodies of the solar system, in the several times of their solar years. Were all the heavenly bodies of the system of the sun like Ptolemy's supposed fixed earth, every one of them would require two suns to produce the solar motions observed from their surfaces. What an occasion presents itself in this view of the solar motions, seen from every body of the solar system, to inspire our admiration of the "Sun" of our salvation. Behold Him, who is limitless in power, using that power in the economy of providing but one sun for the diurnal and yearly illumination of every body of the solar system; and in that very economy there is an exuberance of fullness sufficient for the illumination of a thousand, ten thousand, or millions of revolving worlds.

Origin of the Sun's Motion.

The matter composing the body of the sun was originally free to receive any one right-line impulse to urge the sun forward in the direction of a right line, or to receive one right-line sidewise impulse to simultaneously turn the sun on an axis and urge it forward in the direction of a curve line. The reader will understand, that the right-line sidewise impulse impinging on a globe will always generate rotary and curvilinear motions.

If required to move the sun in the direction of a right line, the force must impinge on the body of the sun in the direction of a line passing directly through the centre of the sun.

From such a motive force, generating but one resulting motion, the sun would be compelled to move forward in a sliding motion in the direction of a right line. But if required to generate the attraction of the gravity of the sun, which is the tendency of his matter to his axial centre, also rotary and curvilinear motions, also the inclination of the axis and his oblate form, a single right-line impulse, directed sidewise and parallel to a line passing through the centre of the sun, was sufficient to produce this wonderful variety of results. And from such a motive force was generated the spheroidal gravity of the sun, his axial and orbital motions, the inclination of his axis, and his oblate form. This miracle of motions, belonging by right as it does to the truths of nature and her law of forces, justly appeals to mankind for the recognition of its divine right ; and though it has so long been hidden from the gaze and understanding of the sons of earthly birth, its lustre shines none the less brilliant.

The Earth.

The matter composing the earth was passed from rest to motion by a single sidewise impulse ; from which arose the gravity of the earth, also its dual axial and orbital motions, also the inclination of its axis and its oblate form.

Suppose a line to pass through the centre of the sun, and extend in space, afterward to be known as the transverse diameter or long axis of the orbit of the earth and the centre of the matter of the earth, and one end of the line to coincide with a point afterward to be known as the perihelion point of the earth's orbit.

Let us, thus prepared, assume that a single side-wise impulse impinges on the matter of the earth (the matter of the earth being between the motive force and the sun) in the direction of a right line, aside from and parallel to the line joining the centres of the matter of the earth and sun, and parallel to and above a plane subsequently to be known as the plane of the earth's orbit, by an amount of angular measurement of 23° 28′, and learn what follows.

1. The one-motive sidewise force started the matter of the earth from an absolute state of rest to a condition of relative motion round an axis, which became the axis of the earth. In this transition, the absolute weight of the matter of the earth passed to its now relative weight, and in this relative weight it tends to the axial centre of the earth, and this tendency is the gravity of the matter of the earth, which was unknown and without existence until the motive force caused the matter of the earth to rotate on its axis; and from the motive force causing the axial rotation originated the gravity of the matter of the earth; which, in the very nature of the case, must be spheroidal gravitation.

2. Also, from the one-motive sidewise force was generated the axial rotation of the earth, and the inclination of the axis is perpetually invariable in each and every revolution.

3. Also, the one-motive sidewise force deflected the earth from a right-line motion, causing it to move forward in the direction of a curve line; which curvilinear motion being continued, resulted in the orbital motion of the earth.

4. Also, because the one-motive force impinged on the earth, at the point before mentioned, the result was the inclination of the axis of the earth, the amount being 23° 28′.

5. Also, from the one-motive sidewise force the matter of the earth, conforming to the centrifugal force of the earth, which was caused by the rotary motion, did take upon itself the oblate form of a sphere.

6. The reasonableness and possibility of the five-fold results mentioned in the previous five observations emboldens me to declare, that the Creator did, by the agency of a motive sidewise impulse, generate the phenomena of motions and resulting forces which belong to any one of the heavenly bodies.

Jupiter.

Again : suppose a line to pass through the centre of the sun, subsequently to be known as the long axis of the elliptical orbit of the planet Jupiter and the centre of the matter of the planet, and one end of that line to coincide with a point afterward to be known as the perihelion point of Jupiter's orbit.

Let us now assume that, in the opening of the epoch of resulting motions, a right-line motive force impinged on the mass of the matter of the planet Jupiter in a line parallel to the line joining the centres of Jupiter and the sun, and aside from it, at a distance of about 45°, but in the plane to become the plane of Jupiter's ecliptic and equinoctial, and then from the force there should arise all the phenomena of resulting motions and forces which belong to Jupiter.

1. The one-motive sidewise force forced the

mass of the matter of Jupiter from its absolute state of rest to a condition of relative motion round the axis of Jupiter, and in the transition the absolute weight of the matter was changed to its relative weight, and in this relative weight it tends to the axial centre of Jupiter, and this tendency is the attraction of the matter of Jupiter, which arose in the matter being precipitated on the axis of Jupiter by the motive sidewise force. Hence the origin of the attraction of gravitation of the matter of Jupiter.

2. Also, the one-motive sidewise force generated the rotary motion of the matter of Jupiter, and this continued rotary motion resulted in Jupiter's axial revolutions.

3. Also, the one-motive sidewise force generated the forward curvilinear motion of Jupiter, which in continuance returned into itself, resulting in the orbital revolutions of Jupiter.

4. Also, the one-motive force generated the position of the axis of Jupiter, which is perpendicular to the plane of his orbit ; the parallelism of the axis will be invariably preserved throughout all his yearly revolutions.

5. Also, the one-motive force generating the axial rotation of Jupiter, his matter, conforming to the centrifugal force, assumed the form of an oblate sphere.

6. Because the one-motive force impinged on the eastern hemisphere of the mass of the matter of the planet Jupiter, the planet Jupiter moves eastward in his journey round the sun, and the question, why Jupiter moves eastward round the sun, and not westward, is answered.

How I wish you would for a moment say I am

right! What a magnificent display of the wonders
of nature would then start into being before you!
You would feel that, at last, the secret of how God
originated the phenomena and resulting forces of
nature is discovered. These wonders of nature
would loom up before you as they never loomed
before.

Not a Copernican-Newtonian astronomer ever
claimed to know why the planets move eastward
round the sun; why the moons of the planets
move eastward round their primaries, except in
one supposed instance; why the comets are confined to no particular direction, but move any way,
eastward or westward, or in any other direction
perpendicular and oblique to the planes of the
planetary orbits. The why is now answered. It
depends on which hemisphere of the heavenly
body the force impinges. If on the eastern hemispheres of the planets, it determines that the yearly
courses of the planets shall be in a course which
the astronomers have named eastward. If on the
eastern hemisphere of the moons, it is determined
that they shall move eastward round their primaries. If on the western hemisphere of a comet, it
is determined that the comet shall move westward
round the sun. Now because the axis of Jupiter
is perpendicular to the plane of his orbit he may
be selected for illustration, to indicate the point of
force from which arises the direction of the heavenly orb. Now, with Jupiter supposed to be before
you, if the one motive force impinge on the eastern
hemisphere of Jupiter, a plane of his axis dividing
the eastern hemisphere from the western, the
course of Jupiter will be eastward round the sun;
but if on the western hemisphere, Jupiter would

be compelled to go forward westward round the sun. Or if the force impinged on the upper hemisphere of Jupiter, which is above the plane of his orbit, Jupiter would be compelled to describe an orbit the plane of which would be perpendicular to the present plane of Jupiter's orbital motion. The direction of a heavenly body, so far as eastward or westward is concerned, or any other direction of a heavenly body, depends on the point at which the sidewise force impinges.

The Moon.

The moon, in motion round the earth and with the earth round the sun, describes epicycles. This kind of orbital motion Newton concluded was due to the mutual attraction of the earth and moon, and the attraction of the sun and moon on each other, conjoined with the moon's projectile forces. Now add the oblique impulse, from which Newton concluded arose the moon's axial motion, and you have a quintuple parallelogram of forces, which were supposed to lie at the foundation of nature's resources to move the moon round the earth, and round the sun, and on her axis.

The Difference.

One right-line motive sidewise impulse sufficed to generate all the known resulting motions and forces of the moon. Of what use, then, for nature to employ five distinct forces? Suppose the matter of the moon to have been gathered at a point which might become a distance of the moon from the earth and a line joining the centres of the two bodies.

If a motive force impinges on the moon in a line parallel to the line joining the centres of the moon and the earth, and aside from it at a distance of between 45° and 90°, the moon would immediately acquire a rotary motion and move forward in a curve line, which, continued, will result in the epicycles which the moon describes in her journey round the earth and sun; and because all the motions and forces of the moon may be produced in a body moving in free space by the agency of a right-line motive sidewise force, it is reasonable to conclude that nature preferred this one force, rather than the received five forces, to cause the phenomena of the moon's motions. The like kind of sidewise forces, used as the Architect of the universe employed them, suffice to account for the motions, even every kind of resulting motions and forces, which belong to the moons of Jupiter, Saturn, Uranus, and Neptune.

Saturn, His Rings and Moons.

The matter of the several parts of the system of Saturn, his rings and moons were arranged, weighed, and their distances from the sun determined, and the interrelations of every part of this system established to be subjected to the dominion of the majestic motive force. In the same instant, Saturn and his rings and moons were projected, by the agency of sidewise forces, from rest to motion, in the companionship of a ceaseless solar journey; and the resulting motions and forces will be maintained perpetually in the system of Saturn, and the rings of Saturn will rotate and go forward in curvilinear motions the same as if they were a part of the body of the planet Saturn and united to him.

ILLUSTRATION.

You may whirl a globe in the same manner that

you whirl a top. There are two kinds of tops—
toys, which boys play with. One kind may be set in
motion by applying the force through the agency
of a string, the other may be set in motion by
the agency of a whip; and if the force is sufficiently
strong and correctly applied, the tops and the
globe will each acquire rotary and curvilinear
motions, and may be seen describing epicycles,
like the moon does, and sometimes the motion
will be in the path of a spiral. Were these
motions produced in free space they would progress continually.

Comets.

The comets, like other bodies of the solar system, were set in motion by the agency of motive
sidewise forces, which generated their curvilinear
motions, resulting in the great varieties of their
elliptical orbits. The most sidewise force that can
impinge on a globe will cause it to move in a
curve line, which, continued, will result in the direction of a spiral. The least sidewise force impinging on a globe will cause it to move in the direction of a curve line, which is the least removed
from a right line. Between these extremes, a sidewise force impinging on a globe is competent to
generate a curvilinear motion of a globe, resulting
in any kind of orbital motion; and therefore, as
far as the requirements of nature are concerned,
the sidewise force is capable of doing more than
nature demands to cause the curvilinear motions
of the celestial spheres. And this exuberance of
motive force is another instance of the opulence of
the resources of nature.

This majestic sidewise motive force binds the
heavenly bodies to pursue their orbital paths, and

leaves no room to fear that bodies, on account of
the possible derangement of the Newtonian forces,
may be thrown out of their present order in creation, and a collapse of the universe ensue.   In
the universe of worlds started into motion, the
sidewise force determined the rates of motion,
and the curvature of the paths resulting in orbits
which should be pursued by the moving bodies ;
and the whole order and arrangement of the
motions of the bodies among themselves can never
permit the colliding of the moving worlds.   The
effect of the sidewise force gives an independence
of motion to every body in the creation.   If the
sun could be removed beyond Sirius, his absence
of light would be felt ; still every planet would
pursue the same path as now.   And if Saturn and
his rings and moons should survive the wreck of
all other worlds, Saturn and his rings and moons
would still pursue the same paths into which they
were originally driven by sidewise forces.   God
put the imprint of his own stability on every moving orb, and the material creation must keep on in
the perfection of motions generated by the majestic motive force until the Creator shall command a
halt in the final desolation of all perishable things.

Motions of Globes.

As I was ruminating, and earnestly desiring to
understand the cause of the being of things, I felt
inclined to the study of the received laws of
motions.   Not a thought of their defectibility had
then entered my mind.   Of what use to doubt
when those glorious mental kings, Benedetti,
Galileo, and Newton, had put their royal signa-
tures to the laws.   Their laws of motions appeared
to be as firm as the throne of Allah, the wonderful

I AM, and the results of his volitions; and the complacent satisfaction which ages of learned men have exhibited in respect to the truth of these laws, seemed to be a guarantee of their immutability. But my assurance of the fidelity of these laws of motion was doomed to be tumbled into confusion.

On a certain day I impressed a globe with a single right-line sidewise force. Judge of my surprise, when at the instant of the impact of the force the globe moved forward, describing a curve line; and but for the resistance of the air and the spheroidal gravity of the earth it would have continued in motion and finished a whole circle of revolution, as the result of a single force! Did my eyes deceive me? Was the globe in an antic of rebellion against natural law? What! a curve-line motion of a body the effect of a single force? Such a thing must be impossible, being contrary to the first law of motion. Newton taught that it could not be; and the united testimony of the learned and intelligent of mankind must not be doomed to reversion, nor the first law of motion lose the dignity of its rank by a single blow or force. What then? Are we to conclude that the globe did move in violation of the first law of motion? Admit this, and then tell why. Can matter move in opposition to natural law? Never! No matter for all the reasons that can be urged against it, the globe did move in the direction of a curve line, and the celebrated first law of motion was powerless to prevent it; and the opinions of mankind should be corrected by it. All hail this born child of curvilinear motion! A single impulse was thine accoucheur; and in the beginning thy kingly power impressed all the glowing orbs of the heavens with the graces of their motions, and to thine imperial rule all matter was subjected. Thy potent force will yet command the scientific world anew to mental toil, its sons and daughters to behold the new and beautiful in celestial motions, and the rapture of pleasure will be such as the natural revelations of nature can only inspire.

The Issue.

Astronomers, mathematicians, and all adherents to the received first law of motion, teach and believe that if a single force impinge on a globe in the direction of a right line, if not otherwise interfered with the globe will move forward in the direction of a right line with the line of the force, and the globe can not move in any other than a right-line motion.

Contrary to this, a right-line force will generate a curvilinear motion of a globe. This reduces the received first law of motion from the rank of an assumed fact to the poverty of a failure in science, leaving the way clear for a better understanding of the doctrine of natural motions.

Law of Natural Motions.

The matter of a globe at rest in free space, would be ready to receive and become obedient to any kind of impulse, to set out in any and every possible direction of right and curve line motions, and the particular direction of the motion of the globe could be determined by the manner of applying the force, and the selection of the point of impact on the surface of the globe.

1. If the force is central, impinging on the globe in the direction of a line passing through its centre,

the globe must move forward in the direction of a right line with the line of the motive force, and encountering no resistance in free and boundless space, the globe would progress in right-line motion continually. From the effect of the central force the globe will move forward in a sliding motion, but without a rotary motion; because this force is powerless to generate any but a resulting single sliding motion.

2. This hypothetical example of right-line motion was possible, but was not employed in the works of nature, because she required, in the execution of her wonderful plan, that all resulting motions should be naturally rotary and curvilinear, and therefore the right-line sidewise force was elected to the rank of ability to do all that the God of nature required to be done in the generation of the phenomena of all resulting motions and forces which belong to all the celestial bodies in the universe.

3. The nearest approach to the motion of a body in a right line is when it is let fall from a hight to the surface of the earth; but then, on account of the very swift motions of the earth, of more than a thousand miles an hour on its axis, and about nineteen miles in every second of time in its orbit, combined with spheroidal gravitation, the path described by the body must be slightly curved.

Rotary and Curvilinear Motions.

Originally the motions of the heavenly bodies were rotary and curvilinear, having been generated by right-line motive sidewise forces, which caused, not only the diurnal and yearly revolutions of the heavenly bodies, but also the inclinations of their axes, their spheroidal gravitation, and the oblate forms of all the celestial bodies.

Let it be noticed that one of the results of the motive sidewise force was the generation of the attractions of the matter of the spheres, and because the curve-line motion of a globe does not depend on some centrally lodged power of gravitation, nature is without occasion to need the intervention of a cause or force like that assigned to the theory of universal gravitation.

And because the attraction of gravitation of matter is spheroidal, if the earth could be placed at the distance of a thousand miles from the surface of the sun, there being no mutual attractions between the two bodies, they would perform their respective functions without the least possibility of being influenced by each other.

Tops.

Sir Isaac Newton says: "A top, whose parts, by their cohesion, are perpetually drawn aside from rectilinear motions, does not cease its rotation otherwise than it is retarded by the air."

Hence the matter of two or one hundred tops rotating among themselves on the earth would not be retarded by gravity, but only by the air. Remove the tops to the free space, where they would encounter no resistance from the air, and they would rotate continually among themselves, having no mutual attractions of their matter.

Suppose the heavenly bodies to be a system of tops (they rotate on their axes like tops), all whirling on their axes, and if tops whirling on the earth escape the effects of the gravity of the earth, the rotating of the heavenly bodies must exempt them also from any kind of mutual attraction. According to Newton, a top, which is an inverted conoid when whirling, is free from all effects of gravitation; and Newton also taught that the rotary motions of the heavenly bodies are entirely free from any of the effects of centripetal force; and these things being admitted, when you learn what is left of the theory of gravitation, as it is taught in the schools, please inform me. The gravitarians never allowed the force of gravitation to exceed the weight of the heavenly body; but the force to cause the rotary motion of a sphere is greater than the weight of the matter of the sphere.

Therefore, if the earth was a homogeneous and perfect sphere, or an oblate sphere, or a prolate spheroid, or a conoid, it would be altogether free from the interference of the assumed force of the gravity of the sun, or of any other body of the system, in any and every part of the orbital journey.

Natural Law.

The laws of nature are absolute, and are so far removed from contingency that the possibility of change in their order or effects is never to be entertained.

On this account, and because the philosophers' first and second laws of motion involve the idea of contingency, and the motions of the heavenly bodies were in no degree originated by them; said laws were found to be misnomers and mere hypotheses. Misnomers being names having origin in misconception, and hypotheses being purely human inventions.

The Received First Law of Motion.

"Everybody perseveres in a state of rest, or of uniform motion in a right line, unless it is com-

4

pelled to change that state by forces impressed thereon."—*Sir Isaac Newton.*

James Ferguson.

James Ferguson, in his *Astronomy,* explained upon Sir Isaac Newton's principles, says: "All motion is naturally rectilineal."

In Parker's *Philosophy,* p. 55, he asks: "In what direction is the motion of a body impelled by a single force?" Answer: "Simple motion is the motion of a body impelled by a single force, and is always in a straight line in the same direction with the force that acts."

At first I thought of what use for me to say anything contrary to what had been taught by geometricians, mathematicians, and astronomers of the Newtonian system of philosophy. With such a host of grand masters to oppose me, I felt the loneliness of my estate and dreaded the encounter; but being urged by an inward impulse which overcame all hesitancy, I advanced tremblingly to the contest, in hope that truth would conquer.

In respect to the names which I have introduced to the reader on the side of right-line motion, it had been good for the men if they had ever seen a body moving in a right line. One such fact, oh, how it would help their laws of motions! And particularly if it had ever happened in nature that a heavenly body was known to have moved in the direction of a right-line perpendicular to the line of the sun's attraction on the body! What man or congress of men, however much they might wish to do so, could ever establish a theory of rectilinear motions, with all nature, in all of her departments, opposed to them? In the annals of time nature, in her boundless congress of things, has given innumerable examples of bodies moving in curve lines, but not one example of resulting rectilinear motion. In the circumambient expanse there are bodies without number; but among the wonderful multitude of orbs which beautify the limitless wilderness of immensity, or atoms flitting in the sun's beams, where was one of them ever seen or known to have moved in a right line?

A right-line resultant motion of a body is forever excluded from the family of worlds, which move within the limits of the outskirts of the material creation, on the frontier line of which many a human thought has often longed to rest, and cast a look of hope toward the home of the holy.

The Received Second Law of Motion.

"The alteration of motion is ever proportional to the motive force impressed, and is made in the direction of the right line in which that force is impressed."—*Sir Isaac Newton.*

"A body by two forces conjoined will describe the diagonal of a parallelogram in the same time that it would describe the sides of those forces apart."—*Sir Isaac Newton.*

This second law of motion is one of those things which have obtained currency among men of science on account of its assumed truth. This law having been raised to the dignity of immutability and numbered with the laws of nature, it appears unwarrantable for any one to question its rank or attempt to ignore its truth.

It will be readily perceived by the reader that the second law, like the first, speaks of right-line motion; and, in addition to this, of a composition of right-line forces, generating a resultant right-line motion in the diagonal of a parallelogram, which

composition is called a parallelogram of right-
line forces.

But the second law of motion can not be true;
for we have seen that in the realm of nature
there is no resultant rectilinear motion, and what
the forces of nature do not produce may be looked
for in vain among the works of art. Therefore,
because in the regions where spheroidal gravity
obtains a resultant motion is of necessity in a
curve line, the body can not describe, by the effect
of the single impulse either side, or by the two
conjoined, the diagonal of a parallelogram. But
you may say, except the force of gravity, and then,
from the composition of the forces, the body will
describe the diagonal of a parallelogram. Is this
the way the very true system, in the person of a
follower of Newton, begs the question? If you
except gravity, you have nothing left that looks
like science. It can not be excepted, for it is
the chief corner-stone of the received system of
astronomy; and if excepted, it shows the poverty
of the forces and how they hobble, resting on
exceptions. Such an appeal is unworthy of a
cause which is supposed to be only and altogether
true.

Gravity of the Sun.

The first law of motion teaches, that a force
impinging on a body will urge it forward in the
direction of a right line. The second law of
motion teaches, that if a force impinge on a moving body it will alter its motion, and the alteration
of its motion will be in the direction of the right
line in which the force is impressed. All right-
line forces, single or compound, will generate only
right-line forces or motions of bodies. Now, if the

second law of motion is in consonance with nature, when the force of the gravity of the sun deflects the earth from the direction of the projectile impulse, supposed to be perpendicular to the line of the sun's attraction, why does the earth move in a curve line, and not in a right line, according to the second law of motion?

Nor does the fact that the force of the sun is attractive, and not projectile, alter the case so as to vitiate the principle involved; for whether the force of the sun attracts the earth, or the earth is driven in the line of the sun's attraction, in either case it is in the direction of a right line, and the result, according to the second law of motion, would be the same.

And because the result of a drawing or attracting force, like that of the sun is supposed to be, is not in any material degree different from a projectile or driving force, those forces, simultaneously acting on a body according to the second law of motion, should compel the earth to describe the diagonal of a parallelogram, two of the sides of which are made up of the lines in which the two forces act at right angles with each other; and in the direction of this diagonal the earth should move, as an effect of the composition of the forces. But the motion of the earth is curvilinear, and not rectilinear; and it must be that the motion of the earth is straight, or else the second law of motion is not a law of nature.

A Difficulty for Astronomers.

It is well known that the parallelogram of forces by which the earth is supposed to be carried around the sun has nothing to do toward causing the rotary motion of the earth. A third force, called an oblique impulse, was called into requisition to account for the revolution of the earth on its axis. In Newton's *Principia* (Book 1, p. 214, cor. 22), he teaches how a globe, by an oblique impulse, may acquire a rotation on an axis which will remain perpetually invariable, and not be subject to centripetal force. It appears, then, that three forces, one attracting and two driving forces, compose the powers that generated the Newtonian manner of moving the earth axially and orbitally around the sun. The two driving forces were supposed to complete their work from the instant of their impact having generated the axial and projectile motions of the earth ; but the force of the sun's attraction was assumed to be constant and perpetual.

The introduction of the third oblique impulse, to originate the rotary motion of the earth, could not have been without the alteration of the curvilinear motion of the earth. For the sake of the subject, let the geometricians, mathematicians, and astronomers, and all others competent to judge, carry out their convictions as to the truth of what they believe to be the attractive force of the sun and the earth's centrifugal force, *a la* Newton, to generate the motion of the earth in its orbit. These forces suffice, you think, to originate the orbital motion ; but an axial motion is also required, and to cause it you must use Newton's third oblique force.

But this third oblique force can not be used against the earth without deranging the curvilinear motion of the earth, and once deranged is to be forever destroyed.

The Zigzags.

In every second of time the earth describes a part of her orbit equal to nineteen miles, and this astonishingly swift curvilinear motion precludes the possibility of its having been originated by the attraction of the sun and the earth's projectile force conjoined. For to suppose that the earth falls in a right line toward the sun at the rate of nineteen miles every second of time, and simultaneously is driven in the right line of the projectile force at the rate of nineteen miles every second of time, the whole course would be a series of zigzag motions, this way and that way, from which the earth could not recover so as to pursue the even and smooth tenor of her way which she is known to do.

There is no escape from these zigzag motions which inhere to the Newtonian forces. If you choose a space of time as small as the one-thousandth part of a second of time, the zigzag motions will still be prominent; and in this time, according to the theory, the earth will describe two sides of a square of one hundred feet, and a motion this way and that way on the square, then the curvilinear motion, and then the oblique force, compose an inexplicable zigzag curve line of confusion. The reader may not be prepared to receive this conclusion, because the resultant confusion looks hardly like anything that could result from the science established by Newton; nevertheless, escape from the sad effects if you can, but let it be an escape in the way of true wisdom.

Incident and Reflected Motions.

The universities and other institutions of learning teach that the angles of incident and reflected
motions of a globe are always equal to each other,
and from this equality there is no escape.   But
it will be made to appear that the angle of the
reflected motion depends altogether on the mode
of the motive force, and that:

1. The reflected motion of a globe may be in
the line of its incident motion.

2. The angles of the incident and reflected motions of a globe may be equal to each other.

3. The incident motion of a globe may be in a
line perpendicular to a wall, and the reflected motion in a line at an angle of many degrees.

4. The incident motion of a globe may be in an
oblique line to a wall, and the reflected motion in
the same line.

Thus demonstrating how much the philosophy
of the schools needs reforming.   I am in some
good degree repeating the epoch of Galileo.   On
one side the learned ability of the intellectual
lights of the nineteenth century, and the consent
of centuries of men of mind, that the angle of the
reflected motion of a globe is always equal to the
angle of its incident motion.   On the other side, a
man, unknown to fame, presumes to teach his
peers of a heaven-begotten, but erring race, that
the angles of incidence and reflection of a moving
globe are equal only when the motive force impinges centrally on the globe ; in all other cases,
when the motive force is sidewise, the angle of
reflection is never equal to the angle of incidence,
which will be clearly illustrated in the following
examples.

DEMONSTRATIONS.

Figure 1.

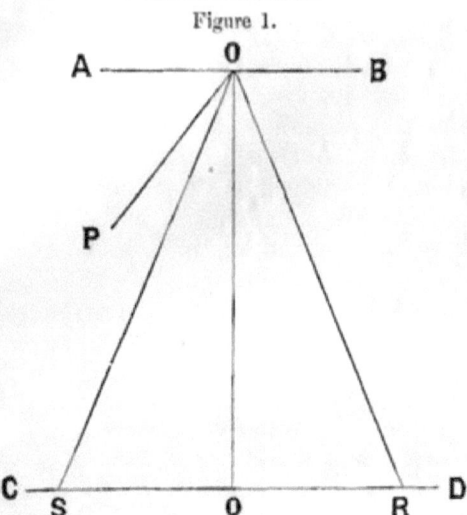

FIRST EXAMPLE.

In Fig. 1, let the line A B represent a wall against which any body may be driven, and the line C D a base line from which bodies may be projected.

1. With a globe at the point O, I applied a central force in the direction of the line O O, passing through the centre of the globe, and the globe from this impulse acquired an incident motion from the point O to O, in the line O O, and in the rebound the globe in its reflected motion moved from O to O, in the line O O. In this example, the incident and reflected motions of the globe were in the same right line O O, perpendicular to the wall A B.

SECOND EXAMPLE.

Again: with the globe at the point O, I urged

against it a motive sidewise force, to the right of,
and in a line parallel to, the line O O, and the incident motion of the globe was in the line O O, but
in the rebound the reflected motion of the globe
was in the line O R.

With the motive force a little more sidewise,
the reflected motion of the globe was in the direction of a line from O to D ; and the sidewise force
could be so applied to the globe at the point O,
that, in its several reflected motions, it would describe every line that could be produced in the
angle O O D.

THIRD EXAMPLE.

I placed the globe again at the point O, and
urged against it a motive sidewise force, to the
left of and in a line parallel to the line O O, and
the incident motion of the globe was in the line
O O, but in the rebound the reflected motion of
the globe was in the line O S.

FOURTH EXAMPLE.

I then placed the globe at the point R, and with
a sidewise motive force to the right of and parallel to the line R O, projected the globe in the line
R O against the point O, and in the rebound the
reflected motion of the globe was in the line O R.
And with the force a little more sidewise the
incident motion was in the line R O, but the
reflected motion was in a line from O to D.

Now when we consider that the reflected motions
of this example, which were respectively in the
lines O R and from O to D, when, according to the
theory, they should in both of the reflections have
been in the line O S, it is plain how far from the
truth is the received theory that the angles of
incidence and reflections are always equal.

FIFTH EXAMPLE.

Again: with the globe at the point R, and the motive force less sidewise than in the fourth example, the globe was projected against the wall at the point O, and in the rebound the reflected motion of the globe was in the line O O.

SIXTH EXAMPLE.

Again: with the globe at the point R, with a motive central force, the globe was projected against the point O, and in the rebound the reflected motion of the globe was in the line O S. In this example, the angle of the incident and reflected motions of the globe are equal.

SEVENTH EXAMPLE.

Once more: with the globe at the point R, with a motive sidewise force to the left of and parallel to the line R O, the globe was projected against the point O, and in the rebound, the reflected motion of the globe was in the line O P.

REMARKS.

In the examples, the sidewise motive forces tended to drive the globe slightly in curve lines, but they were compensated for in the rebound, and were treated in my text as if they were straight-line incident and reflected motions.

1. In the first example, the motive force to move the globe was a central force. From its nature, and the line of its direction being perpendicular to the line A B, the incident motion of the globe progressed in the line O O, and the reflected motion regressed in the line O O.

2. In the sixth example, the motive force to move the globe in the line R O was of the same

kind of central force as that employed in the first example, but the line of its direction, as seen in the figure, is oblique, or inclined to the line A B a measure of several degrees ; and because the force was central, the incident motion of the globe was in the line R O and the reflected motion in the line O S.

3. In the remaining five examples the angles of reflections and incidence are not equal. A most convincing demonstration that when our philosophical fathers gave to the world their notions of forces and the reflected motions of globes they were themselves still in need of more knowledge, and did succeed in making mankind believe that error is truth.

4. In the seven examples I have demonstrated a globe is subject to any variety of angular direction differing from the angle of incidence, or agreeing with it, as the motive force is central or sidewise. Also a motive sidewise force, to drive the globe from the point R against the point O, can be so impressed that in the rebound from O the globe will describe an arc of a circle of which the right line O P may represent the chord.

It is certain that the incident and reflected motions of globes may be in right or curve lines as the motive force is central or sidewise, and therefore they are not the offspring of chance, but arise from and are generated in the natural law of motions, and therefore the reflected motion of the globe may be in the line of projection, as is seen in the fourth example ; or the angle of reflection may be one-half less than the angle of incidence, as is seen in the fifth example ; or the angle of reflection may equal the angle of incidence, as is seen in the sixth example; or the angle of reflection may be more than the angle of incidence, as is seen in the seventh example. Furthermore, a motive force of the central and sidewise kinds will cause globes to rebound just as you have the powers afforded by nature, and the ability to use them; and the power of a certain kind of force to control a globe from the point of its rebound is here brought to light, and the reason for it is found in the law of nature, and it is this: That the matter composing a globe may be subjected to any force that may be impressed on it, not only at the instant of the impact of the motive force, but also at the time of the rebound of the globe, as will be more fully seen further on.

Figure 2.

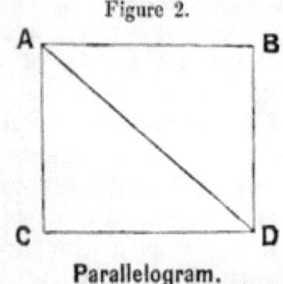

Parallelogram.

You may find the likeness of Fig. 2 in Newton's *Principia*, p. 84, Corollary 1. There Newton teaches: That if a force will cause a body to move in the line from A to B, and another force will move the body in the line from A to C, the conjoining of these forces, impressed on the body at A, will cause it to describe the line A D of the diagonal of the parallelogram A C D B.

This seemingly solid reasoning will baffle every objection which may be brought against it, but one, and that is too much for the paper geometry which has been so long, and often, and every-where, satisfactorily employed to demonstrate the resultant motion which was supposed to arise from the conjoining of two projectile forces.

Newton's universal law of gravity is a third force, according to the theory, which, he said, al-ways acted, and from the interference of its force not even the smallest particle of matter could possibly escape; therefore, whether the body move from A to B, or from A to C, or from A to D, it must encounter the force of gravity, and be deflected from its right-line motions for the very reason that Newton said deflected the motion of the earth from the right line of its projectile force. Why Newton and other geometricians, in their exposi-tions of resultant right-line motions, paid no respect to and made no allowance for universal gravitation, but reasoned as if it had no existence, is singular enough!

The knowledge of the spheroidal gravitation of the earth compels the conviction that a right-line resultant motion of a body in the diagonal of a parallelogram, as the result of two right-line motive forces, never took place; and never can in any region where spheroidal gravitation holds its sway. The fact of the possibility only, to say nothing of its having been done, of causing resultant motion in a straight line is forbidden, and the reason of this is still more fully made out by the considera-tion of the impossibility of composing two right-line forces independent of the force of gravity. Now if to Newton's two motive right-line forces you add his third force of gravity, or, instead of that, you add the force of spheroidal gravity, henceforth none will be found stupid enough to say: That a composition of three forces, two of them being in the lines A B and A C of the figure, will cause a body to move in the diagonal A D of the parallelogram A C D B.

To be Well Understood.

I.

Bodies moving in the air encounter atmospherical resistance, and are also drawn aside by the spheroidal gravity of the earth; but exterior to the atmospheres of all the celestial bodies the space is free, being void of all resistance, and bodies started into motion in this free space, by the effect of the primitive impulse, will move continually; so that when we speak of globes or bodies moving in free space, the reader will do well to have in mind what is the meaning of bodies moving in free space.

II.

If, after all I have said against the Newtonian causes of the celestial motions, my subsequent demonstrations fail to be convincing and satisfactory, the mental training and gain in this pathway of sublime grandeur will more than compensate for the lapsed years of earnest love-sought toil. If defeated and disappointed by the rebut of the truly wise, and the rose-bud of my hope is forbidden to bloom in joyful success, I will retire from the glorious conflict in the possession of the luxury of having wrestled for the mastery with the giant—THE MAN who, in the judgment of the most intelligent of his admirers, is the first in the profundities of science, the greatest geometrician and mathematical naturalist in the line of human beings.

But if I fail, my countrymen, please say I was vanquished with none to share with me the glory of the disappointment.

III.

In my thesis of things I teach that the doctrine of nature, in her motions, is distinguished from right-line motions; and I commend to men, for their adoption, the following formula, which embraces a manner of setting forth a law of nature.

NATURAL LAW OF THE CELESTIAL MOTIONS.

The motions of the heavenly bodies were originally and naturally rotary and curvilinear, which motions were originated by the agency of sidewise forces which were impressed on the bodies in lines parallel to, and more or less aside from, lines passing through the centres of the bodies.

IV.

All the philosophers admit that it is a property of matter to be indifferent to rest or motion. Hence bodies in a state of rest can not move themselves; nor can they, if in motion, arrest their course.

V.

ALTERATION OF MOTION.

The addition of the Newtonian oblique impulse to cause the rotary motion of a globe will cause an alteration of the orbital motion. It makes no difference at what time the oblique force impinges; it will derange the orbital motion and destroy it, compelling the globe to pursue a direction of motion contrary to that orbital motion which is said to have been originated by the Newtonian parallelogram of forces; and on this account, if we had no other occasion, there exists a cause to look for another way of accounting for the celestial motions besides that which is received.

VI.

All bodies possess weight, but their weights are not the causes of their motions, nor any supposed attractions of their weights, else they would have the power to move themselves, which is contrary to nature and educated experience.

But because matter, if moved, must be subjected to a force not resident in itself, but exterior to it, and all the motions, tendencies, and forces pertaining to a moving globe were originated, and may be again, by exterior motive force, I shall be able to demonstrate that all kinds of motions of globes are independent of the Newtonian law of universal gravitation and the received laws of motions.

VII.

Because globes from single motive forces may be urged in any kind of single and compound resulting motions known to exist among the celestial motions, I will attempt to show what kind and direction of motive force will generate the various elliptical, circular, and epicycloidal orbits in which move the sun, planets, satellites or moons, asteroids, and comets.

VIII.

RIGHT-LINE MOTION OF A GLOBE.

So far from it being true, as taught by Newton and Ferguson, the universities and colleges of our country, and throughout the world, that any body, from the effect of a single force, is always compelled to move forward in a right line in the direction of the line in which the force is impressed—*it is never so*, except the impinging force is central, in a line

5

passing through the centre of the globe, and then
the globe, if in free space, or if supported on a
smooth level plane, would move forward in a right-
line motion.

DEMONSTRATION.
Figure 3.

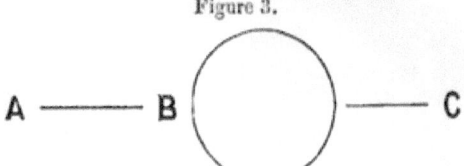

In Fig. 3, suppose the circle to represent a
quiescent globe, its centre and the point B on its
surface to lie in a line with the line A, and the line
A to represent the line of the motive force.

Now, if the motive force is directed in the line A,
and impinges on the globe at the point B on its
surface, the globe will move forward in a sliding
motion in the direction of the right line C.

1. The force to move the globe in a forward
rectilinear motion was a central force, and on this
account the globe acquired a single sliding motion,
but without axial rotation, because it is in the
nature of a central motive force to impart none.

2. This is rigidly true of a globe that might be
so projected in free space, and is true of a globe
supported by a smooth level plane, due allowance
being made for friction incidental to the contact of
the globe with the plane over which it moved. But
if the central motive force is sufficiently strong to
overcome the friction, which it may be, then the
sliding motion will be preserved intact, and so understood, whether in free space or on a level smooth
plane, the globe will move forward in the direction
of a right line in a single sliding motion.

3. Any attempt to move a globe in the direction of a right line, the motive force being not central, is contrary to nature's law of forces, and will meet with a signal failure.

4. Aided by the light of former observations it may now be admissible to infer, that if a globe should be discovered hereafter moving in the direction of a right line it may be taken for granted that it is without an axial rotation, and that the force which generated its motion was a central motive force.

Furthermore, you may infer that all bodies having curve-line motion must have also a rotary motion, for in the laws of nature these resulting motions are inseparable from each other.

IX.

MOTIONS OF GLOBES.

How a globe, subject to a motive central force in a line passing through its centre, may be driven against another globe in a line passing through its centre, and at the instant of colliding the resulting force of the first globe will be transferred to the second globe, compelling it to move forward; but the first globe, having transferred its force of motion, will remain fixed at or very near the point at which the globes collided, as the force was more or less accurately impressed.

But if the force is truly a central force, and properly graduated, the first globe, at the instant of congress with its fellow globe, will remain fixed, and no rebound or turning to the right or left can possibly take place.

DEMONSTRATION.

Figure 4.

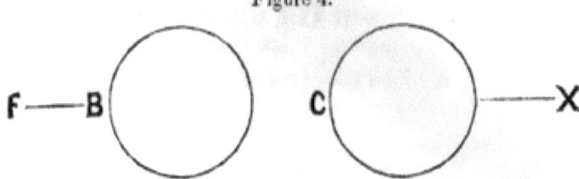

In Fig. 4, suppose the circles B and C to represent globes and their centres, and the points B and C on their surfaces to fall in a right line with the lines F X.

Now, if a motive central force, directed in the line F, impinges on the point B of the globe B, it will be driven against point C of globe C, and at the instant of colliding globe C will move forward in the direction of the line X; but globe B, arrested in its course by the nature of the projectile force at the instant of the colliding, remains motionless.

1. This example shows how the mover of the force may command the motion of the globe after it passed from the motive force at the time of the colliding of the globes.

2. The example shows that a body may have action without reaction. Sir Isaac Newton, on the third law of motion, says : "To every action there is always opposed an equal reaction." This universal portion of the third law of motion I have shown to be without foundation. Under other combinations of conditions and circumstances, action and reaction obtain; but so far as the equality of action and reaction is concerned, it may be equal, or one-half, or nothing, altogether depending on the will of the mover and his choice of the kind of projectile force.

3. What I wished to do was to bring to the light one example of exception to the third received law of motion. . Having accomplished this, I submit the case to whoever, loving truth, may wish to enlarge the domain of his mental perception.

X.

MOTIONS OF GLOBES.

How a globe, from a superior motive force, may acquire a rotary and forward motion, and in its course encounter a second globe, and at the instant of colliding both globes will move forward.

DEMONSTRATION.

Figure 5.

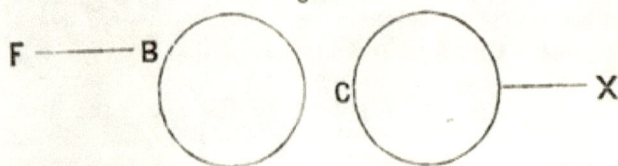

In Fig. 5, suppose the circles B and C to represent globes ready to obey any kind of impulse that may be impressed on them, and the point C on the surface of the globe C to fall in the line X. The line F is the line of the motive force, in which direction the force may be urged against globe B at the point B, which line is above and parallel to a line joining the centres of the globes.

With a motive force in the line F impinging on globe B at the point B, the globe will move forward in the direction of the line X, collide with globe C, drive it forward, and, without being sensibly retarded, follow on after globe C in a compound rotary forward motion. In this example the globe B was impressed by the motive force with a com-

pound rotary and forward motion, which continued
after the colliding of the globes, and this difference
of result, when compared with the former example,
is due also to the will of the mover and his choice
of the location of the force. When the force is applied, as in Fig. 5, on the upper hemisphere of the
globe, I call it a superior motive force, and when
applied, as in Fig. 6, on the lower hemisphere of
the globe, I call it an inferior motive force.

XI.

MOTIONS OF GLOBES.

How a globe, by a single inferior motive force,
may acquire forward and backward rotary motions, and in its advance encounter another globe,
and from the instant of colliding regress with
rotary and backward motions.

DEMONSTRATION.

Figure 6.

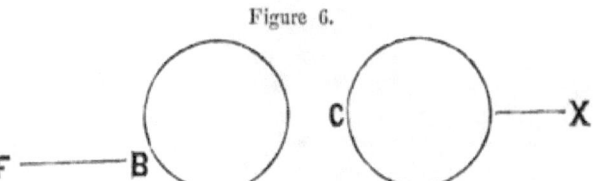

In Fig. 6, the circles B and C represent globes
ready to obey any kind of impulse, and the centres
of the globes and the point C fall in a line with
the line X. The line F is the line for the direction
of the motive force, which line is below and parallel to a line joining the centres of the globes.

With a motive force in the direction of the line
F impinging on the point B of globe B, it will
move forward, collide with globe C, drive it in the
direction of the line X, and from the instant of

colliding with globe C will return over the line in which it was projected, in a compound rotary backward motion.

1. In this case we have an example of the action and reaction of globe B; but the reaction did not originate in the nature of the elasticity of the globe in a rebound, for the rebound, or return of the globe, was wholly at the option of the mover and choice of the force, without any respect to the law of action and reaction, and so far I have demonstrated that the masses of the matter of globes are wholly liable to the action of motive forces.

2. In the first example of motions of globes, under Fig. 4, a central force caused the globe B at the instant of colliding to assume a state of rest.

3. In the second example of motions of globes, under Fig. 5, a superior motive force caused globe B to follow globe C after the colliding of the globes.

Such a direction of force always generates in a globe a compound rotary forward motion, not liable to destruction by colliding with another globe.

4. In the third example of motions of globes under Fig. 6, the inferior motive force was below the centre, and parallel to the plane on which the globe was supposed to move. Such a direction of force will always generate forward and rotary backward motions, not liable to destruction by colliding with another globe, and the three-fold motion may invite and interest the curious to know the capability of the inferior motive force.

XII.

How a globe, by an inferior motive force, may acquire forward and backward rotary motions.

DEMONSTRATION.

Figure 7.

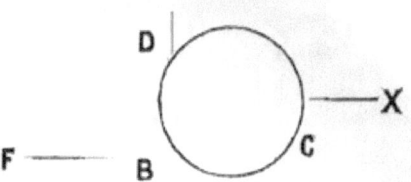

In Fig. 7, the circle B represents a globe in a relative state of quiescence, ready to yield obedience to any mode of force which may be employed by the mover, and move forward in the direction of X, and then retreat over the line of the forward motion, pass the point from which it was projected, and fall back to F.

According to the philosopher's received first law of motion, any body, meeting no obstacle or contrary motive force, will, from the effect of a single projectile impulse, move forward with a uniform motion in the direction of a right line. Contrary to this, it is demonstrable that a kind of oscillatory resulting motion may be generated by a single motive force; and not only so, but that one motive force may be made that will produce the same result that may arise from two motive forces acting against each other in opposite directions in the same right line.

The first law of motion forbids even the rational thinking of such a case as I have proposed; but, somehow, globes, if they were ever subject to the philosopher's laws, have rebelled, and now, in all kinds of directions and in seemingly fantastic curves, in one grand romp of all kinds of resulting motions, declare their freedom from the restraints of the first, second, and third man-devised and erring laws of motion.

With a motive force in the line F of the figure impinging on the surface of the globe at the point B, the globe will acquire a rotary motion in the direction of the letters from C to D and B, and also a forward motion in the direction of X.

The motive force in this example, being an inferior force, will always impart, when impinging on a globe, three resulting motions—rotary, forward, and backward ; but the rotary motion will retard and overcome the forward motion, and then the globe will regress with rotary and backward motions.

These resulting motions constitute a demonstration of the fact, that one inferior right-line motive force will compel a globe to advance and regress in the same right line of direction, doing in this instance what heretofore was supposed to require the operation of two forces.

These advancing and regressing motions may also be caused if the motive force impinge on the globe in Fig. 7 at the point D, in the direction of a line perpendicular to the supposed plane on which the globe may move.

XIII.

RESULTS OF FORCE—DEMONSTRATION.

Figure 8.

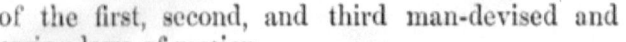

Fig. 8 is supposed to be the segment of a circle drawn on a horizontal plane, and the circle A a globe. The right line, or chord, of the arc is supposed to include a length of twelve feet.

PROPOSITION.

A globe by a single motive force may be made to move in the direction of a chord of an arc, or in the direction of the arc, for the perfect passivity of matter permits all kinds of resulting directions, motions, and forces to be generated by the agency of a single right-line motive force.

First.—Suppose A in the figure to represent a central motive force impinging on globe A in a line passing through its centre. From the effect of such a force the globe will move forward in the direction of the right line, which is the chord of an arc.

Second.—Suppose A in the figure to represent a sidewise motive force impinging on globe A, aside from and parallel to the line of the central force. From the effect of such a force the globe will move forward describing the curve line, which is an arc of a circle.

Third.—This demonstration of the curvilinear motion of a globe opens the way to the true cause of the celestial motions, for if a curve-line motion of a globe can be generated by the agency of one force, of what use to employ two forces, as Newton did, when one force would even answer a more extensive purpose than the mere generation of a curve-line motion?

Fourth.—Furthermore, a single motive force can generate a curve-line motion of a globe. Let us suppose the globe in the figure to have been the planet Jupiter, or any other of the planetary orbs, which at the time of passing from rest to motion had impressed on it such a sidewise force as I have described. From the nature of the force the planet Jupiter would have moved forward in the curve line of Fig. 8, which is now assumed to be an arc of Jupiter's orbit; this curve-line motion being continued, the planet would return to its starting point, and because in free space the planet could not stop, and there being no obstacles in the way, it would continue to describe revolutions, which are the yearly revolutions of the planet. Hence the origin of Jupiter's orbital revolutions is found in a single force; and because the sidewise force generated also a rotary motion in the planet at the same time of the forward motion, the rotary motion being continued, resulted in the axial rotations of Jupiter. Hence the origin of Jupiter's axial revolutions is found in the motive sidewise force; and if such a force might be entertained as the cause of the motions of one of the heavenly bodies, why not of all the celestial spheres?

The Announcement.

It having been demonstrated that a right-line motive force impinging sidewise on a globe will generate rotary and curve-line motions, and that the form of the curve may be of the kind which belongs to a circle, ellipse, or epicycle, I announce to mankind that in the beginning the Creator, by the agency of sidewise motive forces, generated the diurnal and yearly revolutions of the celestial bodies, and that in the nature of things the forces were competent to cause all the known phenomena and resulting forces which inhere in all the heavenly bodies.

1. The sidewise motive force generated a rotary motion, which, being continued, results in the diurnal revolution of the sphere.

2. The sidewise motive force generated a curve-

line motion, the continuance of which results in the orbital revolution of the sphere.

3. The sidewise motive force subjects the matter of a celestial body to its sway, causing its matter to tend to its axial centre, modified by the centrifugal force of the rotating sphere ; and if the measure of the centrifugal force is subtracted from the weight of the matter of the sphere when it was at rest, the remainder will be the measure of the force of the gravity of the sphere.

4. The matter of the heavenly body, conforming itself to the effect of the sidewise motive force, assumed the form of an oblate sphere.

5. The sidewise motive force, in the manner of its application, determined the measure of the inclination of the axis to the plane of the orbit of the heavenly body.

REMARKS.

If you carefully study the laws of motions which were employed by Newton to construct his system of the world, it will clearly appear that for every resultant motion a plurality of forces were required by him to account for the celestial phenomena. Contrast the poverty of the single effect of a Newtonian motive force, with the fruitfulness, even exuberance, of a motive force of nature, and the majesty of the power of a sidewise motive force will justly claim a place in your admiration, and the acknowledgment due to this all-commanding force of nature. When, in the wisdom of God, a power to originate axial and orbital motions, centrifugal and centripetal motions, and the inclination of the axis of a heavenly body to the plane of its orbit was required, his wisdom saw in a single sidewise impulse the power to cause these quintuple results, and matter obeyed the majesty of force, and, up-starting from its rest in countless moving spheres, the resulting motions and forces began a cycle of activities ever interesting to God, men, and angels.

XIV.

Varieties of curve-line motions to which the matter of the heavenly bodies are subjected by single forces.

DEMONSTRATIONS.

Figure 9.

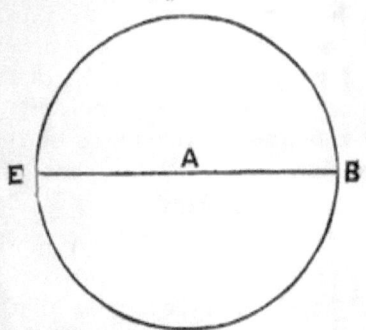

Fig. 9 represents a globe ; the line E B, its equatorial circle ; the line A B, a quadrantal arc or 90°, the first to begin at the point A, and the ninetieth to end at the point B.

1. Between the end of the first degree from A, on to 22° 30′ toward B, a sidewise motive force impinging on the globe will cause it, whether in free space or supported on a smooth level surface, to describe a curve line. The curvature of the line will be least at the end of the first degree, and increasingly greater as the force is directed at the end of the second and third degrees, and so on to the point 22° 30′ distant from the point A. Be-

tween these limits, a sidewise motive force will
generate any kind of curve-line motion, which, returning into itself, will have originated any form of
elongated ellipse which may be required for those
comets, parts of whose yearly journeys are beyond
the orbit of Neptune.

2. A sidewise impulse, impressed successively on
every degree from 22° 30′ on to 45° toward B,
will cause the globe to describe a series of curve
lines, which, returning into themselves, will form
any possible variety of orbits, passing from the elliptical to the circular form, as the motive force is
impressed respectively at the end of every degree.

The orbits generated by the motive force as described, originally impinging on heavenly bodies,
were such as are described by comets whose yearly
journeys are within the orbit of Neptune, and also
the planets and asteroids, and also that that is described by the sun in his orbital journey.

3. A sidewise impulse impressed successively on
each degree from 45° to 90° will cause the globe
to describe a series of curve lines which will partake of the nature of a curve, which is an arc of a
circle; also a variety of curve lines, which form
parts of epicycles and spirals.   Hence whatever
curvilinear direction of a globe is required, the majestic sidewise motive force is competent to the
requirement, and so it was found to be when the
exigencies of the divine purpose required its use in
giving motions to all the worlds.

Billiards.

PROPOSITION.

Because it is a law of nature that the perfect
passivity of matter permits its perfect control by

the will and force of the mover, the motions and directions of motions of billiard balls, nine-pin balls, and base balls are all determined by the mode of the application of the force.

Corollary 1.—Hence the shots and directions of the motions of the balls which are caused by billiard players; and those fancy shots and astonishing directions of motions of balls determined beforehand and unerringly executed by those accomplished masters of the art, Messrs. Dudley Kavanagh, Michael Phelan, and Claudius Berger, are made in the most strict accordance with the law of nature.

Corollary 2.—If the motive force impinges on the billiard ball by the agency of a mace, the ball must move forward in the direction of a right line, because the mace force is the same in nature as the cue central force. But in every cue game of billiards nature asserts her law of the curvilinear motions of globes; but the players, knowing nothing about the law, they concluded they had violated the received laws of motions. The conclusion was just, but only so because the received laws of motions were a rape on nature. Emerge, then, from the wilderness of false philosophy, and in the sunlight of truth henceforth know that the employment of the superior and inferior, sidewise, and oblique forces on which billiard players rely, which never fail them if properly applied, are so far a faithful exposition of natural law!

Corollary 3.—Billiard players have been misguided by the man-made received laws of motions, which, like the idol gods of paganism, have been put in the place of the true law of nature.

Gentlemen of the game, correct your opinions; and may it be your felicity to obey the laws of our

God and Savior as perfectly as the balls you play
with will obey the natural law of force with which
you impress them, for they will always in their
resulting motions move in perfect obedience to
the law of nature, the violation of which, so far as
the motions of globes and balls are concerned, is
absolutely and eternally impossible.

Finally.

Because it is a grand fact and law of nature that
any conceivable kind of direction may be generated
from superior and inferior, central, and sidewise
forces, a globe may be made to move in the direction of a right line or curve line, in the curvilinear
direction of the line of an ellipse, circle, epicycle, or
spiral, in a single or compound motion. But the
motions, if caused in free space, would continue
always, and be more perfect than when executed in
the air or on a smooth plane.

Because the motive sidewise force is sufficient to
account for every known motion of the celestial
bodies, of what use or particular need is there to
employ a plurality of motive forces, as Newton did,
to account for the diurnal and yearly revolutions
of the celestial spheres? Only think of my one
sidewise force to take the place of Newton's three
forces to cause the axial and orbital motions of a
heavenly body!

If, after this, my countrymen doom me to die
unnoticed—Amen! I can afford to wait until MY
TIME COMES! In my long toil to open the way to
reveal the secrets of nature, the nature of the conflict sometimes lashed me with the fury of disappointment, and then, bursting in upon that gloom,
would come the gushing sunlight of hope. At one

time I seemed to see the sons of science, in sullen mood, treating my labors with the go-by, as their fathers had treated my elder brothers in innovation in ages past; and anon, there passed by the souls of the martyrs of science, whose immortal sight had been entranced by the vision of science in her purity, and they pointed to the crown awaiting the man who dared to run, as they had, the gauntlet of strife; and coveting to be numbered with them, I tremblingly advanced toward the goal. Once, wearied almost to death, the whole subject appeared to me to be a lonely wild-goose chase and the flying birds nowhere in view; and then there came a voice from the excellent glory, saying, Child, go forward! and onward I moved once more. This mixed state of alternations was more than enlivened by the assurance of hope that the wonderful and glorious success of leading my nation in paths of knowledge never before walked in by mortals should become a fact made out. In anticipation, the truth-smile of sixty centuries preluded the voice of Nature as she uttered: Now is come the time when mankind learn how God originated the motions of the celestial spheres! The father of the theory of the precession of the equinoxes leading the grand procession of the wise men of the past, the children of science born since his day preceding, came to the grand banquet of triumph in science, and shouted: Glory to the God of nature, for the revelation of the knowledge of his works.

I heard a commotion; it was the stirring of my countrymen to annex, by right of discovery, the cause of the motions of every celestial orb to their mental domain, and Americanize the universe. The stars from every part of the sky looked on the movement in glowing delight, and those star gems on the outskirts of creation waited to welcome the joy; and as my American brethren in acclamation cried, It is accomplished! the nationalities of the whole earth responded, AMEN!

A NEW RESOLUTION

OF THE

Diameters and Distances

OF THE

Heavenly Bodies

BY COMMON ARITHMETIC.

ACCOMPANIED WITH AN

Exhibit of the Variations of the Astronomers,

AND A

DISPROOF OF THE NEWTONIAN THEORY

OF

UNIVERSAL GRAVITATION.

---•••---

BY WM. ISAACS LOOMIS,

Piermont, Rockland Co., N. Y.

---•••---

New York:

T. HOLMAN, PRINTER, CORNER CENTRE AND WHITE STREETS.

1868.

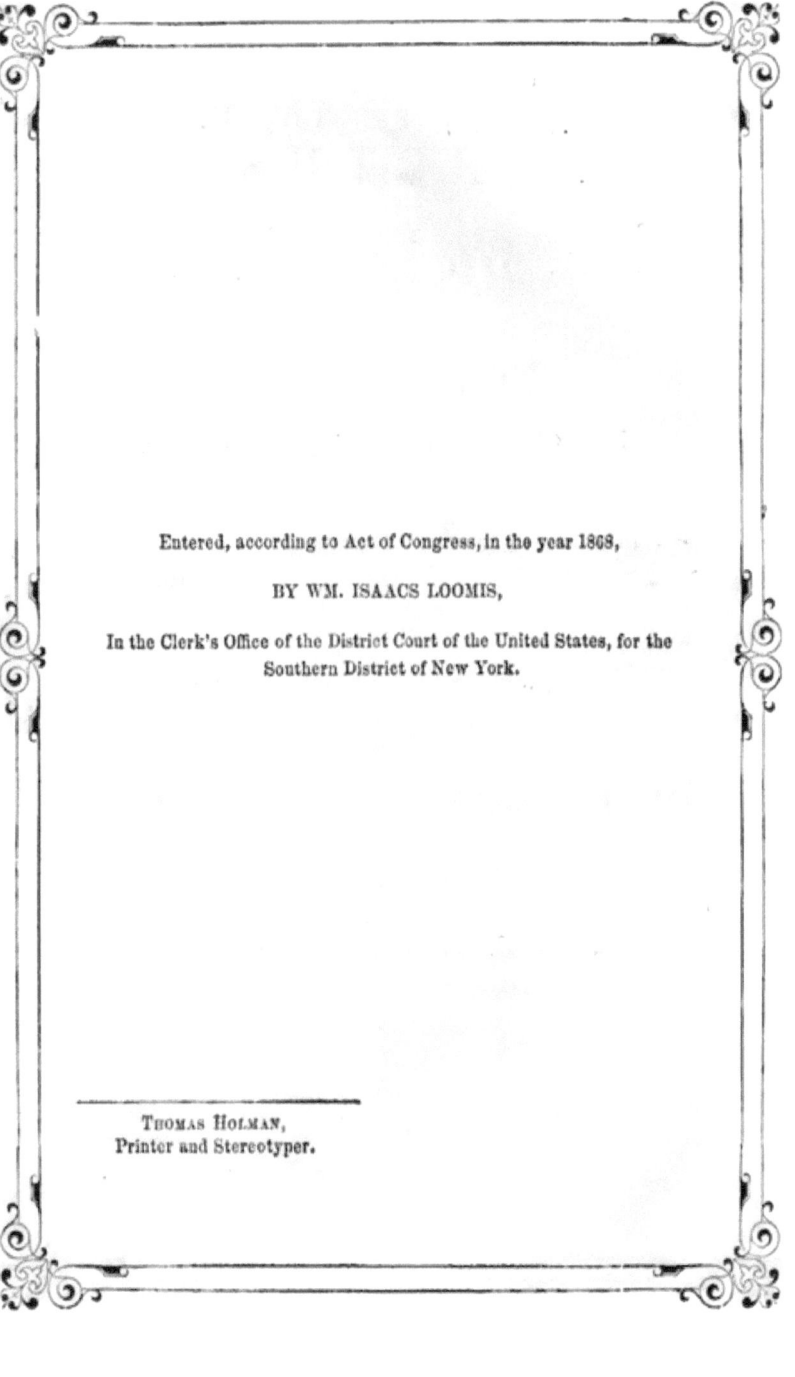

THOMAS HOLMAN,
Printer and Stereotyper.

TRUTHS.

1. "TRUST in the Lord with all thy heart; and lean not unto thine own understanding. In all thy ways acknowledge him, and he shall direct thy paths."

2. Open to men the right path, aided by God-given and God-directed reason, and then the humblest of our race may become familiar with the works of God.

A comparison of my manner of determining the diameters and distances of the heavenly bodies with others.

T. Dick's rule and example to find the real diameter of the moon is given by him in the third volume of his works, on p. 144 of *Celestial Scenery:*

"As radius : is to C G, the distance of the moon, 238,800 miles, : : so is the sine of A C G, 15′ 43″ : to the number of miles contained in the moon's semi-diameter, A G=1091½, which, being doubled, gives 2,183 miles as the diameter of the moon.

$$
\begin{array}{lr}
\text{2d term—C G}=238,800\text{—Log} \ldots & 5.378028 \\
\text{3d term—sine of A C G, } 15' \ 43'' \ldots & 7.660059 \\
\hline
 & 13.038087 \\
\text{1st term—radius} \ldots \ldots \ldots \ldots & 10.000000 \\
\hline
\text{Semi-diameter of the moon } 1.091\tfrac{1}{2}= & 3.038087 \\
\hline
\phantom{\text{Semi-diameter of the moon } 1.091}2 & \\
\hline
\phantom{\text{Semi-diameter of }}2,183\text{''} &
\end{array}
$$

My rule and example to find in the fourth term of a simple proportion the real diameter of the moon:

As the angle of the equatorial horizontal parallax of the moon 57' 5" : is to her apparent diameter of 31' 26" : : so is the base line of the parallax 3,963 miles : to a fourth term in simple proportion in common arithmetic = the moon's real diameter.

Demonstration.—As 57' 5" : 31' 26" : : 3,963 miles : 2,182 miles, which is the moon's real diameter.

Planetary Distance.

After the manner of Kepler, to find the distance of any planet from the sun.

Rule.

Divide the square of the planet's sidereal revolution round the sun by the square of the earth's sidereal revolution, and multiply the cube root of the quotient by the earth's mean distance from the sun. In the use of this rule to find the distance of the planet Mercury from the sun by common arithmetic, or by logarithms, Burritt, on p. 160 of his *Geography of the Heavens*, says : "He need not think himself a *dull* scholar, if by the former method he comes to the true result in FIVE HOURS ; nor remarkably quick, if by the latter he comes to it in *five minutes.*"

N. B.—My distance of Mercury was obtained in less than five minutes by common arithmetic. (See the example on p. 93.)

T. Dick's Moon's Distance by Logarithms.

2d term—3,965=the earth's semi-diameter......................	3.598243
3d term—radius................	10.000000
	13.598243
1st term—sine of 57' 5''	8.220215

M C, distance of moon, 238,800 miles = 5.378028

Moon's Distance by the Author's Method.

As the angle of the moon's parallax of 57' 5'' : is to the circle in degrees 360° : : so is the base line of the parallax 3,963 miles : to the circle in miles 1,499,576, the semi-diameter of which is 238,665 miles, which is the moon's mean distance from the earth. (See my rules on diameters and distances.)

The advantages of my method are : *First*, brevity in operation, astonishingly so, in finding the diameters of the heavenly bodies. *Second*, independent of a knowledge of trigonometry and logarithms, with a very limited knowledge of common arithmetic, these problems to find the diameters and distances of the heavenly bodies may be solved.

Lest any should stumble because my results vary somewhat from those of the astronomers, it may not be amiss to notice the difference between some of the least and greatest diameters of the planets which astronomers have assumed to be very near approximations to the truth.

Sir John W. Herschel makes the diameter of Mercury 156 miles more than Burritt states it to be, and 540 miles more than Ferguson's diameter. Between Ferguson's and Bartlett's estimates of the diameter of Venus there is a difference of 530 miles. O. M. Mitchel's value of Jupiter's real diameter is 11,164 miles more than that given by Ferguson, and 5,164 miles more than Herschel's diameter. E. H. Burritt's computation of the diameter of Saturn exceeds Ferguson's by the enormous sum of 14,952 miles. Sir J. W. Herschel estimated the diameter of Neptune to be 7,890 miles greater than O. M. Mitchel's estimate.

Diameters of Heavenly Bodies.

I will give the angles or arcs, which are the measures of the angles of certain parallaxes of heavenly bodies, their apparent diameters, base line of the parallaxes, and the rule to determine their real diameters by simple proportion.

Moon's angle or arc of parallax....	57' 5"
Sun's " " "	8".6
Mercury's " " "	14"
Venus' " " "	31"
Mars' " " "	16"
Jupiter's " " "	2"
Saturn's " " "	1"
Uranus' " " "	0".4722
Neptune's " " "	0".2967

Apparent Diameters.

Moon's apparent diameter........	31' 26"
Sun's " "	32' 12".6
Mercury's " "	11"
Venus' " "	61".2
Mars' " "	16".61
Jupiter's " "	47"
Saturn's " "	18"
Uranus' " "	4"
Neptune's " "	2".5

The equatorial semi-diameter of the earth is the base line of all equatorial horizontal parallaxes, the linear measure being 3,963 miles.

Rule.

As the angle of the equatorial horizontal parallax of a heavenly body : is to its apparent diameter : : so is the base line of the parallax : to the real diameter of the heavenly body.

Demonstrations.

DIAMETER OF THE MOON.

1. As the angle of the Moon's parallax...................... 57′ 5″ :
   Is to her apparent diameter..... 31′ 26″ : :
   So is the base line of the parallax, 3,963 miles :
   To the real diameter of the moon, 2,182 miles.

DIAMETER OF THE SUN.

2. As the angle of the Sun's parallax, 8″.6 :
   Is to his apparent diameter..... 31′ 12″.6 : :
   So is the base line of the parallax, 3,963 miles :
   To the real diameter of the sun.890,569 miles.

DIAMETER OF MERCURY.

3. As the angle of Mercury's parallax, 14″ :
   Is to his apparent diameter..... 11″ : :
   So is the base line of the parallax, 3,963 miles :
   To the real diameter of Mercury, 3,113 miles.

DIAMETER OF VENUS.

4. As the angle of Venus' parallax, 31″ :
   Is to her apparent diameter..... 61″.2 : :
   So is the base line of the parallax, 3.963 miles :
   To the real diameter of Venus... 7,823 miles.

DIAMETER OF MARS.

5. As the angle of Mars' parallax.. 16″ :
Is to his apparent diameter..... 16″.61 : :
So is the base line of the parallax, 3,963 miles :
To the real diameter of Mars.... 4,114 miles.

DIAMETER OF JUPITER.

6. As the angle of Jupiter's parallax, 2″ :
Is to his apparent diameter..... 47″ : :
So is the base line of the parallax, 3,963 miles :
To the real diameter of Jupiter.. 93,130 miles.

DIAMETER OF SATURN.

7. As the angle of Saturn's parallax, 1″ :
Is to his apparent diameter..... 18″ : :
So is the base line of the parallax, 3,963 miles :
To the real diameter of Saturn.. 71,334 miles.

DIAMETER OF URANUS.

8. As the angle of Uranus' parallax, 0″.4722 :
Is to his apparent diameter..... 4″ : :
So is the base line of the parallax, 3,963 miles :
To the real diameter of Uranus.. 33,571 miles.

DIAMETER OF NEPTUNE.

9. As the angle of Neptune's parallax, 0″.2967 :
Is to his apparent diameter..... 2″.5 : :
So is the base line of the parallax, 3,963 miles :
To the real diameter of Neptune, 33,392 miles.

BY MY METHOD.

The Moon's real diameter is...... 2,182 miles.
    "   Sun's   "   " 890,569   "
Mercury's   "   "   3,113   "
Venus'   "   "   7,823   "
Mars'   "   "   4,114   "

Jupiter's real diameter is	......	93,130 miles.
Saturn's " "	......	71,334 "
Uranus' " "	......	33,571 "
Neptune's " "	......	33,392 "

Distances of the Planets.

1. The sines and tangents of the angles of the equatorial horizontal parallaxes of the sun and planets differ so insensibly from each other, that, without liability to error, the linear measure of the arc of any one of these angles may, without further labor, be assumed to be the same as the linear measure of the tangent of the angle.

2. In the projection of an equatorial horizontal parallax there is exhibited a right-angled triangle, the base line of which is the equatorial semi-diameter of the earth, and its perpendicular leg represents the distance.

3. Because the perpendicular leg of any right-angled triangle is the semi-diameter of a circle, an arc of which is the measure of the angle at the vertex, it is evident that, given the degree and linear measure of the arc of the angle, the perpendicular leg of any right-angled triangle may be determined in the same way that we determine the semi-diameter of a circle, given the degrees and linear measure of an arc of a circle to find its semi-diameter.

Example.

To find the perpendicular leg of a right-angled triangle: Given the angle at the vertex 12°, and the linear measure of the arc of the angle 12 inches.

Demonstration.—As 12° : 360° : : 12 inches : 360 inches÷3.14159=114.59÷2=57.29 inches, which is the linear measure of the required leg.

This method may be employed to find the distances of the heavenly bodies, substituting the linear measure of the base line of the parallax for that of the arc.

Rule.

As the angle of any equatorial horizontal parallax : is to the circle in degrees : : so is the linear measure of the base line of the parallax : to the linear measure of the circle, the semi-diameter of which is the perpendicular leg of the right-angled triangle of the parallax.

Demonstrations.

DISTANCE OF THE MOON.

1. As the angle of the Moon's parallax,   57' 5" :
   Is to the circle in degrees . . . .   360° : :
   So is the base line of the parallax,   3,963 miles :
   To the circle in miles 1,499,576÷3.14159=
   477,330÷2=238,665 miles, which is the moon's
   mean distance.

DISTANCE OF THE SUN.

2. As the angle of the Sun's parallax,   8".6 :
   Is to the circle in degrees . . . .   360° : :
   So is the base line of the parallax,   3,963 miles :
   To the circle in miles, 597,214,853.7209313÷
   3.1415926=190,099,404, which is the diameter of
   the earth's orbit, ÷2=95,049,702 miles, the linear
   measure of the perpendicular leg of the right-angled
   triangle projected in the sun's equatorial horizontal
   parallax, and is the mean distance of the sun from
   the earth.

DISTANCE OF MERCURY.

3. As the angle of Mercury's parallax,   14″ :
    Is to the circle in degrees . . . .   360° : :
    So is the base line of the parallax,   3,963 miles :
    To the circle in miles 366,860,571.4285714, the semi-diameter of which is 58,387,674 miles, and is the distance of Mercury from the earth at the time of his inferior conjunction. Subtract this distance of the planet from the earth from the earth's mean distance from the sun, and the remainder, 36,662,028 miles, is Mercury's distance from the sun.

DISTANCE OF VENUS.

4. As the angle of Venus' parallax,   31″ :
    Is to the circle in degrees . . . .   360° : :
    So is the base line of the parallax,   3,963 miles :
    To the circle in miles 165,678,967.7419354, the semi-diameter of which is 26,368,627, and is the distance of Venus from the earth at the time of her inferior conjunction. Subtract this distance of the planet from the earth from the earth's mean distance from the sun, and the remainder, 68,681,075 miles, is the distance of Venus from the sun.

DISTANCE OF MARS.

5. As the angle of Mars' parallax . .   16″ :
    Is to the circle in degrees . . . .   360° : :
    So is the base line of the parallax,   3,963 miles :
    To the circle in miles 321,003,000.0000000, the semi-diameter of which is 51,089,215 miles, and is the distance of Mars from the earth at the time of his opposition. Add this distance of the planet from the earth to the earth's mean distance from the sun, and the sum 146,138,917 miles is the distance of Mars from the sun.

DISTANCE OF JUPITER.

6. As the angle of Jupiter's parallax,   2″ :
   Is to the circle in degrees.......   360° : :
   So is the base line of the parallax,   3,963 miles :
   To the circle in miles 2,568,024,000.0000000,
the semi-diameter of which is 408,713,720 miles,
and is the distance of Jupiter from the earth at the
time of his opposition. Add this distance of the
planet from the earth to the earth's mean distance
from the sun, and the sum, 503,763,422 miles, is the
distance of Jupiter from the sun.

DISTANCE OF SATURN.

7. As the angle of Saturn's parallax,   1″ :
   Is to the circle in degrees.......   360° : :
   So is the base line of the parallax,   3,963 miles :
   To the circle in miles 51,360,480,000.0000000,
the semi-diameter of which is 817,427,425 miles,
and is the distance of Saturn from the earth at the
time of his opposition. Add this distance of the
planet to the earth's mean distance from the sun,
and the sum 912,477,123 miles is the distance of
Saturn from the sun.

DISTANCE OF URANUS.

8. As the angle of the parallax of
         Uranus...................   0″.4722 :
   Is to the circle in degrees.......   360° : :
   So is the base line of the parallax,   3,963 miles :
   To the circle in miles 10,876,848,793.0000000,
the semi-diameter of which is 1,731,105,871 miles,
and is the distance of Uranus from the earth at the
time of his opposition. Add this distance of the

planet from the earth to the earth's mean distance from the sun, and the sum, 1,826,155,573 miles, is the distance of Uranus from the sun.

DISTANCE OF NEPTUNE.

9. As the angle of the parallax of
    Neptune ....   0''.2967 :
    Is to the circle in degrees ....   360° : :
    So is the base line of the parallax, 3,963 miles :
    To the circle in miles 17,310,576,339.7371028, the semi-diameter of which is 2,755,063,855 miles, and is the distance of Neptune from the earth at the time of his opposition. Add this distance of the planet from the earth to the earth's mean distance from the sun, and the sum, 2,850,113,557 miles, is the distance of Neptune from the sun.

Solar Distances of the Planets.

Mercury's solar distance....		36,662,028	miles.
Venus' " "	....	63,681,075	"
Earth's " "	....	95,049,702	"
Mars' " "	....	146,138,917	"
Jupiter's " "	....	503,763,422	"
Saturn's " "	....	912,477,123	"
Uranus' " "	....	1,826,155,573	"
Neptune's " "	....	2,850,113,557	"

The distances of the heavenly bodies may be found by Division. I will exhibit two examples.

Rule.

Divide the linear measure of the tangent of the angle of the parallax by the circular measure of the arc of the parallax, and the quotient will be the term required.

Distance of the Moon by Division.

1. The circular measure to seven places of decimals of the arc of the angle of the moon's parallax of 57' 5" is 0166048.

2. The linear measure of the tangent of the angle of the parallax, with seven ciphers annexed, is 3,963.0000000.

Demonstration by Division.— 3,963.0000000÷0166048=238,665 miles, which is the moon's mean distance.

Distance of the Sun by Division.

1. The circular measure to twelve places of decimals of the arc of the angle of the sun's parallax of 8".6, is 000041693976.

2. The linear measure of the tangent of the angle of the parallax, with twelve ciphers annexed, is 3,963.000000000000.

Demonstration by Division.—3,963.000000000000 ÷000041693976=95,049,702 miles, which is the sun's mean distance. Compare these results with the mean distances of the sun and moon, found by a different process on p. 92.

1. I have demonstrated how to find the diameter of any one of the heavenly bodies in the fourth term of a single proportion.

2. I have shown how to determine the linear measure of the perpendicular leg of a right-angled triangle in the same way employed to find the semi-diameter of a circle, thus bringing within the reach of all a way to find the distances of the heavenly bodies by common arithmetic.

3. By a very simple process in Division, I have resolved the distances indicated by the parallaxes of the moon and sun.

Circular Measure.

A circle, whose radius is unity, the circular measure of its circumference retaining twelve places of decimals, is 6.283185307179=360°.

The circular measure of an arc of one degree is 0.017453292519.

The circular measure of an arc of one minute of a degree is 0.000290888208. The circular measure of the arc of the parallax of any one of the heavenly bodies may be found, and the distance indicated by the parallax be determined by division, as in the given examples.

My ambition in this department of science is satisfied. I had most earnestly desired, longed for, and labored to bring the solutions of these astronomical problems within the reach of all who understand common arithmetic. Having accomplished this, I leave it to others to extend, by a little modification of my rule, the principle of finding the unknown perpendicular leg of any right-angled triangle, the linear measures of whose sine, arc, and tangent disagree in consequence of the largeness of the angle.

The Stars are without Parallax.

A near and fixed object will suffer no apparent displacement when viewed from a mere point (like it would if viewed from the extremities of a line); and ten or ten thousand observations from the same point would all be in the line of the visual ray of the first observation. So it is in all observations made to determine stellar parallaxes. They are all in the line of the same visual ray that was first directed to a star to find its distance, and, therefore, for the want of a line whose longitude would subtend an appreciable angle, the stars are of necessity without appreciable parallax.

1. On p. 6, I have given the resulting distance of a star's annual parallax of 1″ of a degree. The assumption shows that the distance to the nearest star can not be less than nearly forty trillions of miles, and how much further who can tell, for the stars, as it respects the annual motion of the earth, are without variableness, having no shadow of turning.

2. The whole diameter of the earth's orbit, if compared with the line of a star's distance, is a mere point; but the astronomers make the base line of their annual parallaxes but one-half of the diameter of the orbit of the earth, and consequently but half a point. Now a mere point is without length, breadth, or thickness, being without assignable quantity; and strange that but half of an unassignable quantity is the chosen base line of the astronomers. This being so relatively true, the marvels of the astronomers' parallaxes of the stars, if true, involve a greater marvel, that, from a series of observations made from the extremities of but half a point, certain stars have been found to have a very appreciable quantity of parallax in angular measurements, varying from 0″.046 to 0″.915.

3. That the assertion, "the whole diameter of the earth's orbit, when compared with the distance of a star, dwindles to a mere point," may be implicitly received as true, Burritt says: "The whole diameter of the orbit of Saturn (1,824,915,246 miles) is no thicker than a spider's web when compared with the distance of the stars."

The Examination.

From what I have written, before I presented this portion of my work to be thought of by men, there can be : *First*, no mutual gravitation of the heavenly bodies among themselves. *Second*, for the want of this mutual gravitation of the celestial spheres, the theory of the precession of the equinoxes is without the ratification of nature. *Third*, the time and revolution of the sidereal year of the sun is baseless. *Fourth*, by the testimony of nature I will be able to establish the fact, that our earth, which is an oblate spheroid, revolves around the sun after the manner of a homogeneous and perfect sphere revolving around the sun, the density of its matter not affected by the force of its axial rotation. *Fifth*, the variations of the astronomers are wonderful ; and that the disciples of Newton, who are among the most highly gifted of the sons of earth, should have been so much out of the way, affords cause for a deliberate inquiry : What is truth ?

But before we engage further in the grand conflict, it will, without doubt, be pleasant to my readers to know that the system of astronomy which originated with Copernicus was enlarged and improved by Sir Isaac Newton, and expounded, to the wondering delight of intelligent men and women, from age to age, is, by its friends and admirers, thought to be unimpeachable, and its collections of dogmas synonymous with a collection of the facts of nature. The words of Ferguson, Herschel, and Dick will best set forth their views.

1. In Ferguson's *Astronomy*, p. 41, he says : "Sir Isaac Newton has established this system on such an everlasting foundation of mathematical

and physical demonstration as never can be shaken, and none who understand him will hesitate about it."

2. Herschel, in his *Outlines of Astronomy*, p. 19, says : "There is now no danger of any revolution in astronomy like those which are daily changing the features of the less advanced sciences."

3. In Dick's works, Vol. III., p. 25, he says : "The system broached by Copernicus, notwithstanding much opposition, soon made its way among the learned in Europe. It was afterward powerfully supported by the observations and reasonings of Galileo, Kepler, Halley, Newton, La Place, and other celebrated philosophers, and now rests on a foundation firm and immutable as the laws of the universe."

Now, not believing that the shaking of the Copernican system of astronomy is the same as shaking the true facts of nature, I advance in my work, and hope, as I have often prayed on this subject, to aim for the right way and the gain of the truth, and God defend and prosper me.

"Precession of the Equinoctial Points."

PROPOSITION.

Through the earth's annual motion round the sun, the stars seen from our earth do not change their points of rising, and the theory of the precession of the equinoxes teaching they do, the testimony of nature is to be accepted; and as such a phenomenon could only arise from the fact of the earth preserving the invariability of its equinoctial points, I infer from this testimony of nature that there is nothing in nature to warrant the conclusion that the equinoctial points fall back, there is no "regress of the earth's nodes."

The amount of the precession of the equinoxes is said to be 50".1 of a degree every year; and were the theory as much a fact of nature as it is supposed to be by learned astronomers, the stars would change their points of rising 50".1 of a degree every year; and a star, which in A. D. 1858 rose in the plane of the celestial equator, would in A. D. 1868 rise 8' 21" east of the celestial equator. But a star, and all stars which this year describe the circle of the celestial equator, and circles parallel to and declining to either side of it, describe the same diurnal circles which they appeared to do last year, or ten years ago. This unanimous verdict of the invariability of the whole starry host, is nature's decisive refutation of the theory of the precession of the equinoxes.

The Pseudo Sidereal Year of the Sun.

Webster, under the word year :—" *Sidereal year;* the time in which the sun, departing from any fixed star, returns to the same. This is 365 days, 6 hours, 9 minutes, 9.6 seconds."

The astronomers and lexicographers are unanimous in their opinions as to the time and existence of their sidereal year of the sun, but the times of the real and apparent revolutions of the heavenly bodies fully demonstrate the fallacy of the so-called "sun's sidereal year." At a time when the centres of the earth, sun, and a star are in a straight line, let the time and revolution of the apparent yearly sun begin by the star, and because of the apparent diurnal motion of the stars in the time of 23 hours, 56 minutes, 4.09 seconds, at the close of the time of the yearly revolution, when the centres of the earth, sun, and star should be in the same straight line, the star will be advanced $92° +$ beyond the line. Hence, because the time of the astronomers' sidereal year of the sun is not a multiple of the time of the apparent diurnal revolutions of the stars, their sidereal year of the sun exists not in nature.

The Pseudo Sidereal Revolution of the Earth.

Because the stars have apparent diurnal motion, and the time of the yearly revolution of the earth is not a multiple of the time of the diurnal revolutions of the stars ; all revolutions of heavenly bodies based on a fixed star are false.

In Herschel's *Outlines of Astronomy*, p. 202, he says : "The annual retreat of the equinox is 50″.1, and this arc is described by the sun in the ecliptic in 20 minutes, 19.9 seconds. By so much shorter is the periodical return of our seasons, than the true sidereal revolution of the earth round the sun."

But the earth does not set out from a star in its journey round the sun; the effect on the stars being the same as if the orbital motion had no existence, and therefore Herschel's "true sidereal revolution of the earth round the sun" is nothing more than his aberration from the facts of nature.

The Cause of Kepler's Failure.

It is known to all informed, that the sun and stars have perpetual apparent motions. When Kepler set about to found his sidereal revolutions of the planets, he excluded from his calculations the perpetual apparent diurnal motion of the stars, assumed their fixedness, and then from a fixed star laid the foundation for his sidereal revolutions of the planets. This exclusion of the apparent motion of the stars led to a false system ; and being contrary to nature, the revolutions must be also contrary to nature, having no place but in the assumption. Therefore, when Sir Isaac Newton, in his *Principia*, p. 388, says, "The periodic times with respect to the fixed stars," he is perpetually contradicted by the perpetual apparent motion of every star in the celestial sphere.

Variations of the Astronomers.

1. T. Dick says: "The effect of the regress of the equinoctial points, is to cause an apparent revolution of the stars around the poles of the ecliptic."

2. Mattison, in his *High School Astronomy*, p. 70, says: "The distant stars have no motion, real or apparent, around the poles of the ecliptic."

3. The reader will observe, that what Dick affirms, Mattison denies.

4. Burritt's *Geography of the Heavens*, p. 29, says: "In consequence of the motion of the earth eastward in its orbit, the stars appear to have a motion westward."

5. Mitchel's *Popular Astronomy*, p. 77, on the orbital motion of the earth, says: "Now the earth's centre in the space of one day and night, or during one rotation, actually passes over 2,000,000 of miles; and it would seem as though this change of position would sensibly affect the return of our star to the meridian; but such is the vast distance of the stars, that visual rays sent to the same star from the extremities of a base line of 2,000,000 of miles in length, are absolutely parallel under the most searching instrumental scrutiny that man has been able to make."

6. What Burritt affirms, Mitchel denies.

7. Webster, in his *Spelling Book*, p. 144, says: "The earth turns every part of its surface to the sun once in twenty-four hours." Suppose Webster to have opened a school among the Indians of the far north, who had not seen the sun for more than a month. He informs his pupils that the learning of centuries has culminated in demonstrating the fact of the earth turning every part of its surface to the sun once in twenty-four hours. After such an announcement, who of the company would appear to be the most stupid—the great American lexicographer, or his pupils? They might inquire what earth is meant; for surely this part, occupied by us, has not seen a ray of the sun for more than thirty times twenty-four hours. Contrary to this, the earth turns every part of its surface to the sun once in the time of 365 solar days, 5 hours, 48 minutes, 48 seconds, and as is the difference between the time of a solar day and solar year; so great is the mistake of Webster.

8. Burritt teaches: "The earth moves eastward in its journey round the sun."

9. Dr. T. P. Jones, in his *Conversations on Natural Philosophy*, p. 105, says: "The earth moves westward in its journey round the sun."

10. In the mental romp led on by Humboldt, in his *Cosmos*, Vol. I., p. 88, he says: "Light travels one distance of Sirius in three years."

11. Peters says: "The distance of Sirius from the earth is so great, that the time required for its light to reach us is fifteen years."

12. Mitchel's *Planetary and Stellar Worlds*, p. 211, says: "Stars of the first magnitude send us their light in about seventeen years." Among the stars of the first magnitude Sirius is numbered.

13. "Henderson reached the conclusion, in his observations on Sirius, that it required twenty-one years and nine months for the light of that star to reach the earth."

14. From among the big thoughts I select: "Huyghens assumed the intrinsic brightness of Sirius to equal the sun."

15. O. M. Mitchel says: "Sirius is the brightest and probably the largest of the fixed stars, with a diameter of more than a million of miles."

16. Wollaston says: "Sirius is equal to sixty-three suns."

17. Humboldt says: "Arcturus is equal to 1,331 suns."

18. Herschel says: "The star Vega in Lyra is thirty-eight times the diameter of the sun, and its solid contents 57,872 times greater."

19. Mattison outdoes these liliputian calculations by saying: "The star 61 in the Swan is estimated to be 200,000,000 of miles in diameter." Not far from being 10,000,000 times larger than the sun.

20. In Humboldt's *Cosmos*, Vol. IV., p. 120, on the sidereal revolutions of the planets, he says: "During such a revolution a planet passes through exactly 360° in its course round the sun;" and in this conclusion all astronomers rest.

21. In Webster's Dictionary, under "*Tropical Year*,—The period occupied by the sun in passing from one tropic, or one equinox, to the other. On account of the precession of the equinoxes, it is 20 minutes, 20 seconds, shorter than the sidereal year;" and in arc, according to Herschel, 50".1 of a degree less than 360°. In this difference all the astronomers are agreed.

22. The difference among the advocates of the sidereal and tropical revolutions of the sun is not calculated to produce a conviction of the infallible nature of their science, as will be made to appear, in that Ferguson and Burritt give to the apparent sun the same number of degrees in his tropical revolution that is given by Kepler, Newton, and Humboldt to a planet or the sun in their sidereal revolutions.

23. In Ferguson's *Astronomy*, p. 152, he says : "The sun describes the whole ecliptic, or 360° in a tropical year." It should be 50".1 of a degree less than 360°.

24. In Burritt's *Geography of the Heavens*, Part II., p. 114, he says : "The sun describes the whole ecliptic, or 360°, in a tropical year." It should be 50".1 less than 360°. Thus confounding the sidereal and tropical revolutions in degree. If the science had been true, the advocates were in these things mistaken, for the tropical revolution in degree should be 50".1 of a degree less than the sidereal revolution ; but they were engaged in expounding a mere theory, as is abundantly evidenced by the variations adduced.

25. As there is no two returns of the centre of the sun or that of the earth to the same fixed star in the time in which the earth passes through exactly 360° of orbital revolution, the sidereal, tropical, and equinoctial revolutions of the astronomers in time and degrees are confusion ; and their confounding the tropical and sidereal revolutions with each other in degree gives no illumination to their infallible scheme, which they supposed consisted of a transcript of the facts of nature.

Parallelism of the Earth's Axis.

1. The earth is an oblate spheroid, and being carried around the sun by the effect of an original sidewise impulse, and not by the sun's assumed attraction, revolves as if it were a homogeneous and perfect sphere, maintaining the invariability of its equinoctial points and the constancy of the poles of the heavens.

2. The line of the earth's axis prolonged to the sphere of the stars is the axis of the heavens, around which the stars appear to revolve ; and in whatever part of its orbit the earth may be in, at either solstice or equinoctial point, the axis of the earth will coincide with the axis of the heavens.

3. To this definition Herschel rigidly adheres in his *Outlines of Astronomy,* p. 192, for he says : "In this annual motion of the earth its axis preserves at all times the same direction, as if the orbital motion had no existence, and is carried around parallel to itself, and pointing always to the same vanishing point in the sphere of the fixed stars."

4. From this absolute parallelism Herschel, not nature, departs in his *Outlines of Astronomy,* p. 172. He says : "It is found, then, that, in virtue of the uniform part of the motion of the pole, it describes a circle in the heavens around the pole of the ecliptic as a centre, keeping constantly at the same distance of 23° 28' from it, in a direction from east to west, and with such a velocity that the angle described by it in this, its imaginary orbit, is 50″.10."

5. In Herschel's *Treatise on Astronomy,* third edition, p. 169, he says : "The bright star of the Lesser Bear, which we call the Pole Star, has not always been, nor will always continue to be, our

cynosure; at the time of the earliest catalogues it was 12° from the pole; it is now (1835, date of the edition) only 1° 24', and will approach yet nearer."

6. For the next twenty-four years the distance remained constant; for in Herschel's *Outlines of Astronomy*, fourth edition, p. 173, he says: "The bright star of the Lesser Bear, which we call the Pole Star, has not always been, nor will always continue to be, our cynosure; at the time of the construction of the earliest catalogues it was 12° from the pole; it is now (1859, date of the edition) only 1° 24', and will approach yet nearer." So that, according to the statements of Herschel, from the time of the earliest catalogues to 1835 the distance between the pole of the heavens and the bright star of the Lesser Bear was diminished 10° 36' by a constant departure of the earth's axis from its parellelism. But from 1835 to 1859 the distance was the same, preserving the parellelism of the earth's axis for a period of twenty-four years.

7. In Rollin's *Ancient History*, Book I., p. 141, he says: "The poles of the heavens have remained the same for a period of three thousand years."

8. Herschel teaches that the poles of the heavens go forward, as an effect of the precession of the equinoxes.

9. Ferguson, in his *Astronomy Explained on the Principles of Sir Isaac Newton*, says: "The poles of the heavens, as an effect of the precession of the equinoxes, fall backward." Place these extremely opposite motions of the same pole of the heavens along side of Burritt and Jones's opposite motions of the earth, and the faith and reason which will comprehend how the earth can move backward and forward in its orbit at the same time will have

no trouble in explaining how the motion of the poles of the heavens can, at the same time, be invariable, and in motion, in opposite directions.

Proposition.

The earth revolves around the sun the same as if it were a homogeneous and perfect sphere. If the Newtonian law of universal gravitation, admitted, as we will see subsequently, to be the weakest of all forces of attraction, the superior forces of the motion of the heavenly spheres would absolve them from all allegiance to the sun's attraction. For the better understanding of the argument, I am willing to admit the existence of all Newton claimed for his discovery, and then show that the mutual attractions of every atom of matter, and of the mass of every sphere, tends to a perfet equilibrium.

Hypothesis.

Suppose a homogeneous and perfect sphere, of a consistence not to be molded into the form of an oblate spheroid as an effect of axial rotation, of the size of the earth as nearly as may be, revolving around the sun as an effect of the assumed attraction of gravitation of the sun.

According to Newton, there being no redundant matter gathered at the equator of such a globe, its nodes will not regress, and its axial rotation will not be acted on by centripetal force, as is the case with an oblate spheroid.

1. Seen from the surface of such a globe following the earth round the sun, during the time of one or one hundred orbital revolutions, the stars will preserve the invariability of their points of rising, culminating, and setting.

2. It is identically so with the stars seen from

our earth. The star watchers have kept their intense gaze on the rays of the twinkling stars, and eagerly sought to know: Do the stars change their points of rising from day to day, from year to year? And to every inquiry, they have given an invariable shining, No; never.

3. The same conclusion was reached by O. M. Mitchel, in his *Popular Astronomy*, p. 18: "An examination of the points of rising, culminating, and setting of the fixed stars, showed them to be absolutely invariable." Therefore, because the stars seen from the earth never change their points of rising, culminating, and setting, which phenomenon is authenticated by O. M. Mitchel, this fact of nature is a demonstration that the earth moves round the sun, the same as if it were a homogeneous and perfect sphere.

4. The position of the earth when at one or the other of the equinoctial points, if the sun's attraction of gravitation affects the earth, the attraction must be the same on the northern hemisphere that it is on the southern hemisphere, resulting in a perfect equilibrium, the same as if the whole matter of the earth was absolutely balanced on its centre, preserving the parallelism of the axis and the constancy of the poles of the heavens. So when the earth is at either equinoctial point, the action of the gravity of the sun is the same as if the earth were a homogeneous and perfect sphere.

5. The equatorial diameter of the earth equals 7,926 miles, and its polar diameter 7,900 miles. Within the earth you may describe a perfect sphere, every diameter of which equals the earth's polar diameter. The excess of matter above the contents of this perfect sphere is thirteen miles, thick at the

circumference of the equator, declining gradually from either side of it to both the poles, at which points it is 0. This excess of matter constitutes the difference between a perfect sphere and an oblate spheroid, and on it (sometimes called the redundant or superabundant matter gathered at the equatorial regions) Newton supposed the attraction of the sun acted to cause the equinoctial points to regress. This involves the novelty of the sun's attraction being greatest on small quantities of matter, and least on greatest quantities of matter. Thus prepared with the quantities requisite to understand the subject, suppose a ring of matter, of the consistence and mass of that portion of the earth included in the difference between its polar and equatorial diameters, revolving around the sun, having the inclination of its axis the same as that of the earth.

The equinoctial points of such a ring will, according to Newton, be continually regressive.

Then at some distance from the ring, with a swifter motion, suppose a homogeneous and perfect sphere to be revolving around the sun, of a size to fit within the ring, having the same inclination of axis with the ring. .

Of such a sphere Newton says, in *Principia*, p. 214, Book I. : "And the inclination of the axis, or the velocity of the rotation, will not be changed by centripetal force." The sphere overtakes the ring, passes into it, and when the equator of the sphere touches the equator of the ring, they adhere, and instantly the force of the attraction of gravitation on the sphere to preserve the parallelism of its axis, assisted by the additional force of its axial rotation, overcomes the very small force of the attraction of gravitation on the ring to cause the regress of its equinoctial points, and henceforth, in the union of the ring and sphere, the now spheroid will move round the sun the same as if it was a homogeneous and perfect sphere.

Corollary 1. The precession of the equinoxes assumes that the attraction of gravitation is stronger on that part of the earth thirteen miles deep at the equatorial regions, diminishing to 0 at the poles, than it is on the contents of the sphere within it, whose diameter is 7,900 miles. This is unreasonable.

Corollary 2. The precession of the equinoxes supposes that the force of the attraction of universal gravitation is more on one pound of matter of that part of the earth which constitutes its oblate form of matter, than it is on ten pounds of matter of its spherical contents under the same law ; and this proportion being much greater in relation to the matter of the earth, which gives it its oblate form, compared with the enormous amount included within the sphere whose diameter is 7,900 miles. By so much is the absurdity greater.

Corollary 3. If the force of this attraction of universal gravitation on the shell of an egg is more than it is on the contents of the egg within the shell, we may accept the Newtonian hypothesis that the shell of the earth (called so by Herschel) composing the oblate form of the earth, is more strongly attracted than the rest of the earth. But the hypothesis is so contrary to reason, lacking the verifications of nature, as to demand its exclusion from the pale of science.

The Tides.

When the matter of our earth was started into motion round its axis, the forces to cause the tides were generated. The centrifugal force to cause the rise, and the centripetal force to cause the fall, of the waters. Hence the origin of the tides, and all observed true phenomena may be traced to the centrifugal and centripetal forces of the earth, every atom of its matter being perpetually subjected to these forces in the given case.

On this affirmation I rest, in the consciousness of its entire truth; for as I have demonstrated that all the known forces of nature pertaining to a heavenly body may be generated by a single impulse, it results that nature, in her works, is independent of the dogma of universal gravitation.

An Antic of Universal Gravitation.

It is assumed that from a given point the waters of a distant sphere may be urged in opposite directions.

According to Sir Isaac Newton, the attraction of every particle of the matter of a sphere may be assumed to be lodged in the centre of the globe, and on this hypothesis let the centres of the earth, moon, and sun be in a straight line, the moon being between the earth and sun, and the mutual attractions of the three bodies exerted in the line of the conjunction of the earth, moon, and sun.

From the centre of the earth in this line the attractions of the sun and moon are said to draw the waters of the earth toward them, causing a high tide on the side of the earth nearest to the sun and moon; and the same attractions of the sun and moon are supposed to project in an opposite

direction from the centre of the earth the waters,
causing a high tide on this opposite side of the
earth.   But the assumptions involving, as they do,
the theory that the whole of the attractions of the
sun and moon in a given line may both pull and
push a part of the matter from the centre of a
third distant sphere in opposite directions, is an
antic indeed, and too contrary to true wisdom to
find a place in true philosophy.   On one side of
the earth there may be a high tide, in the time of
the entire absence of the sun and moon, they for
the time being on the other side of the earth ; and
if on one side, why not on the other, for like
causes produce like effects, and our conclusion is
adverse to the received theory.

Apparent Stellar Motions.

The disciples of Newton and Copernicus are at
fault in ascribing as an effect the apparent daily
acceleration of the stars to the annual motion of
the earth.

In T. Dick's works, Vol. III., p. 19, under the
caption, "Annual Motion of the Stars," speaking
of the changes which the clusters of stars undergo
from time to time, he says : "Those variations in
the appearance of the stars lead to the conclusion
that there is an apparent annual revolution of
these luminaries."

In Burritt's *Geography of the Heavens,* p. 29, he
says : "In consequence of the earth's motion eastward in its orbit, the stars seem to have a motion
westward beside their apparent diurnal motion."
This apparent annual revolution of the stars, like
the apparent yearly revolution of the sun, T. Dick
says, is due to the "annual revolution of the earth

around the sun." This conclusion is also maintained by Burritt. That the astronomers were
mistaken is made out in a most conclusive way by
an appeal to the facts of nature.

The amount of the mean daily acceleration of
the stars westward is 59′ 10″.68+, but the amount
of arc which the earth describes in its mean daily
motion in its orbit is 59′ 8″.33. Hence the arc or
angle described by the stars in their mean daily
acceleration is 2″.35+ more than the arc described
by the earth in its mean daily motion in its orbit.
On this account, when the astronomers attribute
the cause of the apparent yearly motion of the
stars to the motion of the earth in its orbit, they
stand impeached for want of the true knowledge
of the facts of nature.

Cause of the Stars' Daily Acceleration.

An arc of the celestial equator appears to pass
the meridian in the time of a mean solar day, equal
to 360° 59′ 10″.68+, and but 360° in the time of a
sidereal day.

By using the time (24 hours) of a mean solar
day as a standard of measurement, take the time
of some mean midnight, with a star on your meridian, and at the time of the next mean midnight
the star will be advanced beyond your meridian
westward an amount of angular measurement equal
to 59′ 10″.68+. So from one mean midnight to
another in the time of 365 mean solar days, by
these arcs of 59′ 10″.68+, the stars will move eastward presenting all the phenomena described by
Dick in the time of 365 mean solar days, or which
is the same, the time of 366 sidereal days, which is
in time 6 hours, 9 minutes, 9.6 seconds less than

the time of the astronomers' year of the earth by the stars.

If you were to determine the revolutions of the earth on its axis by a star, every time the earth made one exact revolution on its axis, the stars would finish a complete apparent sidereal day revolution around the axis of the heavens; but when you extend the standard of time to that of a mean solar day, in consequence of it the stars will have a mean daily acceleration of 59' 10".68+ westward around the axis of the heavens, in addition to 360° of apparent revolution arising from the motion of the earth on its axis, the same as in their diurnal motion.

Therefore, the observed apparent annual motion of the stars, in the time of 365 solar days, is composed of the arcs of the mean daily acceleration of the stars, belonging to effects of the earth's axial motions transferred to the stars and mixed up with the diurnal motions, and may be made plain by the following:

1. The continual motion of the earth on its axis will cause the stars in appearance, to an observer, to have continual motion.

2. If you take the time in which the earth makes one rotation on its axis, and make this, as the astronomers have done, a standard of time; then, counting the revolutions in consecutive order, the stars will appear to have consecutive diurnal revolution around the axis of the heavens, each consecutive revolution in the exact time in which the earth completes a revolution of 360° on its axis.

3. But if you, as before stated, take the time of a mean solar day, and periods of from midnight to midnight, to watch the stars and conform their mo-

tions to the standard of time, the mean daily accelerations of the stars will give them a westward motion every day, increasing by the addition of an arc of $59' 10''.68+$, resulting in this: That if on the mean midnight of your own selection you find a star on your meridian at the next midnight, it will be advanced westward $59' 10''.68+$, and in the lapse of 365 solar days the star will be on the meridian again.

The astronomers have made a mistake in not noticing that the time of a mean solar day, if applied to the stars, would generate their apparent mean daily acceleration; but attributing it to the mean daily motion of the earth in its orbit, and not perceiving it to arise from the motion of the earth on its axis for the time of a mean solar day, they left the way open for me to show the true way to the children of men.

Law of Planetary Motion.

The planets do not go round the stars like they do round the sun. On this account, when the area of the orbit of the planet is known to be a mere point when compared with the stellar distances, the effect of the orbital motion of the planet on the stars is the same as if the orbital motion had no existence. This agrees with the appearances of nature, and, therefore, the number of the apparent revolutions of the stars ($366\frac{1}{4}$) seen from the earth will be one less (equaling the number of axial rotations) than the number of the revolutions of the earth for the time of its solar year, which are $367\frac{1}{4}$, exactly the number of times the earth turns on its axis by a star, and revolves round the sun.

The Astronomers' Annual Parallaxes.

In the Smithsonian Report for 1858 p. 135, is given certain parallaxes, varying from 0″.915 of a degree, to 0″.046 of a degree. The Smithsonian Report is not inferior in authority and correctness, so far as it moves in concert with all institutions of learning; but I prefer to quote and refer to it, rather than any other, because the Institution was originated as a specialty for the diffusion of knowledge among men. I especially invite the very particular attention of the President, Officers, Board of Regents, and the learned Secretary of the Smithsonian Institution to a careful examination of my claims, lest others of their countrymen, less honorable in fame and position, step in before them in acknowledging the facts of God in nature.

Bessel's Annual Parallax of 6l Cygni, is 0″.348.

(*From Smithsonian Report for* 1858, p. 135.)

Those who accept this parallax as probably true, should take enough interest in the subject to learn that the given distance indicated by it in the Report, instead of being equal to the distance over which a ray of light would move in 9.4 years, should be nearly 19 years. All the astronomers' parallaxes are vitiated by a like quantity, in consequence of their bisecting the isosceles triangle projected in the parallax, taking but one-half of the base line, without correspondingly reducing the measured parallax a like quantity.

If a star seen from the extremities of the diameter of the earth's orbit suffers an apparent displacement of 2″ of a degree, the distance indicated by it would be about twenty trillions of miles. But if you bisect the isosceles triangle, and take the semi-

diameter of the earth's orbit for the base line, and
also for the angular subtense of the parallax, as is
done in the Smithsonian Report for 1858, p. 132,
the resulting distance will be about twenty trillions
of miles, the same as when the conditions involved
the whole of the diameter of the earth's orbit for
the base line of 2″ of parallax. But I propose the
true and whole diameter of the earth's orbit to be
used as a base line of an annual parallax, as defined
by Webster, and from its extremities it is assumed
that a star seen had an annual parallax of 1″ of a
degree, and trigonometrically, or by my new
methods by simple proportion and division, the result will be the same, about forty trillions of miles,
or twice as much as is given by the astronomers.
This is what I mean when I say that the manner
of the astronomers in bisecting their annual parallaxes lead to but half the true result.

Now, I have given an annual parallax of 1″, and
if you will, you may bisect the isosceles triangle of
the parallax after the manner of that to which I
have referred you in the Smithsonian Report ; and
also bisect the angle of the parallax which was
subtended by the diameter of the earth's orbit,
and the result will be, as before, about forty trillions of miles, twice as far as the men of science
have heretofore thought the distance of the stars
was from an annual parallax of one second of a
degree. I will now particularly notice Bessel's
annual parallax of 61 Cygni, it being 0″.348 of a
degree. Wishing to place the argument on the
most solid foundation, becoming the dignity of the
subject and the fame of the discoverer, I will place
before the reader what is said about the base line
of annual parallaxes in the Smithsonian Report for

1858, p. 132 : "Our change of position, involving a distance of more than 200,000,000 of miles, dwindles down to nothing in comparison with the line which extends from the earth to the stars." Admit this, and then the base line of Bessel's parallax was nothing, and the parallax must have been 0″.000 also.

Axiom.

The star 61 in the Swan was observed from a mere point, and such observations culminated in a point ; and hence any amount of an appreciable parallax, when the extent of field of observation admitted of no other extension than could be afforded from a mere point, was impossible.

When, in addition to this, you take into consideration that Bessel's observations of 61 Cygni were at all times complicated by the diurnal and supposed annual aberration of the light of the stars, by the assumed precession of the equinoxes, the nutation of the earth's axis, the refraction of light, and the deflection of the light of the stars as it enters our atmosphere, the probabilities of the truth of his parallax have vanished away.

Peters' Annual Parallax of Capella is 0″.046.

The annual parallax of the star Capella, by Peters, printed in the Smithsonian Report for 1858, p. 135, is 0″.046 of a degree, and the time required for its light to reach us is said to be 71.7 years.

The Difference Between Theory and Facts.

A parallax of 0″.046 of a degree, seen from the extremities of the diameter of the earth's orbit, indicates a distance forty-two times greater than that of Herschel's annual parallax of 1″ of a degree, as set forth in the fourth edition of his *Outlines of Astronomy*, p. 456, and light would require a period of over 140 years to pass over the distance. Reduce the line of the diameter of the earth's orbit to a yard, and Herschel's resulting distance from a parallax of 1″ of a degree in the same proportion, and their relation to each other is as one yard to sixty miles nearly.

Again : with the diameter of the earth's orbit reduced to a yard, and the distance indicated by Peters' annual parallax of the star Capella in the same proportion, and the relation they bear to each other is as one yard to 2,520 miles. This analysis clearly aids ordinary minds to readily perceive that these things being so, the proportions at once lead to the conclusion that all such annual parallaxes are merely theoretical.

Does not this comparison place the annual parallaxes in so forlorn an estate as to render their acceptance as facts of nature impossible, they appearing more like impositions in science than beautiful developments of natural truth ?

1. The parallax of the star Capella indicates a distance of over 850,000,000,000,000 of miles, which is about twice the distance allowed for in the Smithsonian Report.

2. The distance indicated by the parallax of the star Capella is forty-two times greater than Herschel's annual parallax of 1″, and is twice the quantity allowed for in the Smithsonian Report.

3. Light is known to travel at the rate of 192,000 miles each second of time, and at this rate it would require over 140 years for the light

of the star to reach the earth—twice as long as is allowed for in the Smithsonian Report.

4. Because visual rays directed from the extremities of the diameter of the earth's orbit to a star, supposed to be 19,788,239,040,000 of miles from the earth, will coincide and be the same with respect to the star, it becomes a monstrosity in science to suppose that at forty-two times the distance the visual rays of the observer will cross each other, and subtend a parallax of $0''.046$ of a degree. Or you may discount the half of the calculation, and get down to that of the Smithsonian Report, and the same fact concerning the law of distance cuts off all hope of obtaining an annual parallax. You may make another discount of one-half, and get far below the calculation of the Smithsonian Report, and still there comes, from the profound, unfathomable distance, no hope for annual parallaxes.

Universal Gravitation.

In the Smithsonian Report for 1856, p. 200, it says : "Newton's theory of universal gravitation : the most extended generalization ever established by man. It may be expressed as follows :

" 1. The attraction exists between the atoms of all matter at finite distances, and is the same for all kinds of matter ; hence,

" 2. The force of attraction is proportional to the mass of the attracting body, the distance being the same.

" 3. If the same body attracts several bodies at different distances, the forces are inversely as the square of the distances.

" All deductions from this theory are in strict

accordance with the phenomena of nature. The only proof of the truth of any physical law."

At this point I join issue with the scheme, and say: Because the truly understood phenomena of nature is in strict disaccordance with the deductions from the theory of universal gravitation, it can not be true. And because the assumed attraction of the sun is capable of carrying around the sun in orbits as many bodies as can be placed side by side, in as many orbits as can be described in the bounds of the system of the sun, this repletion is too much for the theory as heretofore expounded to endure; and this being too much, exposes its own fallacy.

The Assumed Quantity of the Sun's Attraction.

The force of the attraction of the sun has been estimated to be between five and seven hundred times more than all the forces of all the other bodies of the solar system; but I am prepared to prove that the sun is as capable of carrying a number more than a thousand times greater than all the bodies which are now assumed to be carried round the sun by his own attraction, as he is capable of carrying Mercury alone by the theory.

Extent of the Sun's Attraction.

From every point of the surface of the sun radiating into space the light of the sun goes forth, extending beyond the orbit of Neptune, the light decreasing in intensity as the square of the distance increases.

So the attraction of gravitation from every point of the surface of the sun, it is said, goes forth, and extends beyond the orbit of Neptune, decreasing in intensity as the square of the distance increases,

and thus it appears that the disciples of Newton
hold that a like law which obtains in nature in respect to the light of the sun, holds good in respect
to their assumed dogma of the attraction of the
gravity of the sun.

Furthermore, you are not to suppose that the
mutual gravitation of a planet and the sun are
gathered up and follow the planet round the sun ;
but like as a body or planet moves in the vast field
or ocean of the sun's light, or like a fish moves
through the water, or a bird moves through the
air, so a heavenly body moves through the vast
field of the sun's attraction of gravitation, which
has been assumed to be coequal with the extent of
the light of the sun, and governed by the same law
of the square of the distance.

You are also to conclude that the sun's attraction of gravitation is not arrested by the density of
a heavenly body, as the light of the sun is ; but, according to the theory, it passes through a body,
however dense it may be, with as much freedom
as if the space occupied by the planet was free from
every obstruction, and to suppose otherwise, would
in the event of a conjunction of all the planets,
tumble the theory of universal gravitation into in-
extricable confusion.

Illustration.

Divide the area of the orbit of the earth into as
many angles or parts as may be subtended by the
equatorial diameter of the earth, seen from the
centre of the sun. In every one of these angles or
parts the attraction of gravity of the sun is supposed
to be always present, the same as is the sun's light,
the former to move the earth, the latter for its illu-

mination, without any respect to the presence or absence of the earth. All of the Newtonian philosophy are free to admit the sufficiency of the force of the sun's attraction to carry the earth over any one of these angles or parts, in the earth's journey through the vast ocean of the attraction of gravitation; and if so, why not sufficient to carry a globe of the size and mass of the earth, placed in every one of these angles in a revolution round the sun? In this attraction of the sun on the planets, the astronomers have perpetrated a darling error in assuming to weigh the sun against the planets on an imaginary steelyard or balance, and on such a basis they have computed the weight of the bodies of the solar system, and made it the measure of the mutual attractions of all the bodies revolving around the sun. Admit the astronomers' law in this case, and at a time when the planets are in conjunction, if then they can be weighed against the sun, by the same reasons a like experiment may be tried on the opposite side of the sun with another imaginary steelyard or balance, and another set of planets like those first weighed, and the result must be the same. So you may project as many radii from the sun's centre to the outmost bounds of the solar system as the circular space will admit of, to accommodate the diameters of the planets. Use these radii as imaginary steelyards or balances, place on every one of them bodies exactly like the planets, of the same number, and simultaneously they may all be weighed against the sun without any more disturbing his force or position than would the weighing of the planets alone against the sun, and with the same imaginary result.

Now select one of the angles into which the area

of the earth's orbit was divided, and let it be the one
beginning with the vernal equinoctial point ; and as
the earth moves out of this angle, the force does not
move along with it, but remains in the angle, and
is as potent to move a second and third earth following the first as it was the first one. So on add
globe to globe in consecutive order, until the sun is
surrounded with a ring of globes of the size and
density of our earth, and the force of the sun's attraction to cause the orbital motion of the earth is
also sufficient, because of its abiding force over the
whole orbit, to carry this ring of globes round the
sun in continual orbital motion. Deny this, and
you deny the doctrine of universal gravitation.
Call to mind the spherical space illuminated by the
sun, the outskirts of which are far beyond the orbit
of Neptune, and at every point within it there is
assumed to be continually present some force of
the sun's attraction, as intense as when at first the
primordial laws of the universe were called into
requisition by the Creator. Some have thought
that Mercury is as dense as lead, and the planets
outward are decreased in density, so that the density of the matter of the planet Neptune equals the
density of cork. With some such scale of decreasing density over the square of the distance from the
sun, suppose at every point within the solar system an atom of matter to be present, and the atoms
free to move among themselves. Now let every
one of these atoms of the density of lead at Mercury's distance, decreasing to the density of cork at
Neptune's distance, from the sun, be subjected to
the Newtonian projectile and centripetal forces, and
for the reason, if it be the sun's attraction that carries the planets around the sun, the same force is

sufficient to carry every one of these atoms round the sun, because the force of gravitation in unwasted energy is assumed to be ever present at every point of the spherical space of the solar system. This is so much more than the system of weighing the sun against the planets can endure, that it, and all that is related to it, should be abandoned for a better way of knowledge.

Universal Gravitation.

The Smithsonian Report for 1856 defines the attraction of gravitation to be, "(46) The reciprocal tendency of all parts of the solar system to approach each other;" and, "(50) Gravitation the most feeble of all attractions."

1. Of the bodies of the solar system this can not be true, because the forces of the axial and orbital revolutions of the spheres are greater than the calculated gravitation of the spheres among themselves.

2. On p. 18 there is an experiment to show how a certain quantity of matter may or may not be under the action of the gravitation of the sphere. Such is the nature or effect of axial rotation, that any forces exterior to the rotating heavenly body are abundantly overcome by it, securing the stability of the motion of the body.

3. All error carries with it the seeds of its own dissolution, the means of its own refutation. The admission that the force of gravitation is the most feeble of all attractions, is weakness indeed. Weakness to such an amount as is worthy to be lost sight of in calculating and accounting for the forces of nature to move the heavenly bodies, unless you assume that a weak force overcomes a stronger one, which is absurd.

The Crown in View.

(*Smithsonian Report for* 1856, p. 201.)

" (52) The earth is nearly a sphere, and all bodies fall in straight lines, directed nearly to its centre."

What a fruit of cultivated ignorance, and the evidence of how the noble in intellect servilely follow tradition! There was a time when, on the descent of bodies, the students of nature were divided in opinion ; some claiming that all motion was originally and naturally curvilinear ; and others, that all motion was naturally and originally rectilinear. This latter opinion, though contrary to nature, prevailed ; and now, without a true why or wherefore, even the learned Secretary of the Smithsonian Institution avows this error for truth, when all the phenomena of nature, THE ONLY PROOF OF THE TRUTH OF ANY PHYSICAL LAW, are opposed to his teaching.

That bodies do not fall in straight lines, directed nearly to the centre of the earth, or as others teach, directed exactly to the centre of the earth (for the scholars are not agreed), is demonstrated by the fall of meteors, and also by the descent to the earth of all kinds of projectiles, they universally and invariably describe curve lines in their descent, being subject to the forces of the earth's motions, from the force of which they can not escape. And because in the phenomena of nature there is no true record of the observed right-line motion of any body, the law of straight-line motion, taught in the Smithsonian Report, is not consonant with the facts of nature, and therefore not true.

The hypothesis of universal gravitation endows

every atom of matter with power to move itself.
This is contrary to nature, matter being alike indifferent to rest or motion, its perfect passivity being
originally necessary to permit of its being moved;
and when started into motion around the axis of
each one of the heavenly bodies, then, and not
before, arose the attraction of the matter of the
sphere to its axial centre. Hence the origin of
the gravitation of the matter of each one of the
heavenly bodies; and being confined to the sphere
and its atmosphere, the natural, proper, and signifi-
cant name of it is Spheroidal Gravitation.

This spheroidal gravitation, in its effects, was
seen by Sir Isaac Newton, but not understood by
him; and hence, instead of attributing the descent
of bodies to the earth, and the tendency of every
particle of the matter of the earth, to the attracting
tendency of the earth's axial rotation, the earth's
true centripetal force, he supposed an unseen
power, to himself, as he confesses, perfectly incom-
prehensible, to draw all the particles of the matter
of the earth to its centre. He then stamped every
particle of all the matter in the universe with this
mistake, and originated his now universally received doctrine of universal gravitation. Had he
known that from a single impulse a globe could be
urged in the direction of a curve line, some of the
labor of the *Principia* would have been expended
in another theory of the celestial motions.

I have shown, on p. 73, that from a projectile
impulse a globe may be urged in the direction of
a curve line; and such a demonstration led me to
the conclusion, that the same kind of force would
turn a planet on its axis, and urge it forward over
an arc of its orbit; and because the curve-line

motion of a globe arising from a single impulse
may be more or less curved, so as to agree with
the curve of any circle, ellipse, or epicycle, it became evident to me that all the directions of
motions and varieties of orbits in which the
heavenly bodies are known to move were originated by single impulses, and these discoveries
originated the right, the authority, and duty to
say to mankind : Behold the way of the Lord in
nature !